About the Author

Laurie Faria Stolarz was raised in Salem, Massachusetts, and educated at Merrimack College in North Andover. She has an MFA in creative writing and a graduate certificate in screenwriting, both from Emerson College in Boston. She currently teaches writing and French, and is working on the sequel to *Blue Is for Nightmares*. Visit her website at www.lauriestolarz.com.

To Write to the Author

If you wish to contact the author or would like more information about this book, please write to the author in care of Llewellyn Worldwide and we will forward your request. Both the author and publisher appreciate hearing from you and learning of your enjoyment of this book and how it has helped you. Llewellyn Worldwide cannot guarantee that every letter written to the author can be answered, but all will be forwarded. Please write to:

Laurie Faria Stolarz
% Llewellyn Worldwide
P.O. Box 64383, Dept. 0-7387-0391-5
St. Paul, MN 55164-0383, U.S.A.
Please enclose a self-addressed stamped envelope for reply,
or $1.00 to cover costs. If outside U.S.A., enclose
international postal reply coupon.

Many of Llewellyn's authors have websites with additional information and resources. For more information, please visit our website at:

http://www.llewellyn.com

Blue is for Nightmares

Laurie Faria Stolarz

2003
Llewellyn Publications
St. Paul, Minnesota 55164-0383, U.S.A.

FIRST EDITION
First Printing, 2003

Book editing and design by Rebecca Zins
Cover design by Gavin Dayton Duffy
Cover image (texture) © Digital Stock
Cover image (candle) © Stockbyte
Developmental editing by Megan C. Atwood

Library of Congress Cataloging-in-Publication Data
Stolarz, Laurie Faria, 1972–
    Blue is for nightmares / Laurie Faria Stolarz.—1st ed.
        p. cm.
    Summary: Sixteen-year-old hereditary witch Stacey Brown has nightmares of her roommate being murdered and hopes that her magick will be enough to pro-tect Drea—unlike the last person whose death Stacey dreamed.
    ISBN 0-7387-0391-5
    [1. Witchcraft—Fiction. 2. Magic—Fiction. 3. Stalking—Fiction. 4. Schools—Fiction. 5. Extrasensory perception—Fiction.] I. Title.

PZ7.S8757B1 2003
[Fic]—dc21
                                                                          2003047612

Llewellyn Publications
A Division of Llewellyn Worldwide, Ltd.
P.O. Box 64383, Dept. 0-7387-0391-5
St. Paul, MN 55164-0383, U.S.A.
www.llewellyn.com

Printed in the United States of America

One

They're always the same. Always at night, in the forest, looking for Drea. The sound of his body lurking some-where behind me. Branches breaking. Leaves crackling. Wind whirring in my ears, watering my eyes. And the pain in my stomach—sharp, raw, scathing. Real.

My nightmares make me dread sleep.

I pinch the safety end of the razor blade between three fingers to write. Then I grab the virgin candle and carve the initials *D. O. E. S.* into the rounded side, tiny flakes of sparkling blue wax crumbling from the surface with each incision and every drag of the blade.

They're Drea's initials, but she doesn't suspect a thing, just keeps scribbling away in her diary, like any other night, sitting up in her bed, only a few feet away.

With the last curl of the *S*, I place the razor to the side and pluck a branch of sage from the drawer. It's perfect for burning, all dried up—the leaves shriveled, twisted and gray. I wind a piece of string around it for a cleaner burn, so it won't be as smoky, so I'll have less chance of getting in trouble. Then I drop it into the orange clay pot by my bed.

"Going to bed?" Drea asks.

"In a few." I unscrew the cap off the bottle of olive oil and pour a few droplets onto my finger.

She nods and yawns, caps her feather-tipped pen, and closes up the diary. "Just do me a favor and don't burn the dorm down. I have a serious history presentation tomorrow."

"All the more reason," I joke.

Drea and I have been roommates for a little over two years, so she's used to rituals like this.

She rolls over onto her side and pulls the covers up to her chin. "Better not stay up too late. Don't you have a French test tomorrow morning?"

"Thanks, Mom."

I watch as she closes her eyes, as her lips settle for sleep, as the muscles around her forehead loosen and relax. It's sickening. Even after midnight, with no visible trace of makeup, not a smidgen of cover-up, hair knotted up in a rubber band, she still looks perfect—angled cheeks; salmon-pink, pouty lips; loopy, golden hair; and cat-shaped eyes with curled, jet-black lashes. It's no wonder why every guy at Hillcrest wants her, why every girl hates her—why Chad keeps coming back, even after three breakups.

I touch the top end of the candle with my oily finger. "As above," I whisper. Then I touch the bottom. "So below." I wet my finger with more of the oil and touch the center surface. I drag my finger upward, return it to the center, and then drag it downward, careful to keep the carved letters pointed in my direction so she won't see.

"Wouldn't it be easier just to wet the whole thing at once?" Drea asks, her eyes, open, watching me.

I turn the candle counterclockwise, blocking the letters with my palm, and continue moistening the circumference in the same fashion. "Probably, but that would confuse the energies."

"Of course," she says, rolling over. "How ignorant of me."

When the candle is fully anointed, I light it with a long, wooden match and place it on the silver holder my grandmother gave me before she passed away. It's my favorite holder because it was hers and it's sort of dishlike, with a curly handle that winds around the base.

I close my eyes and concentrate on the waning moon outside, how it's an opportune night to make things go away, how the sage and the engraved candle will help. I light the branch and watch it burn; the leaves curl up and dance in the orangy-yellow flame, then turn black and disappear, the way I pray my nightmares will.

When the sage is no more than ashes, I carry the clay pot over to the corner sink and fill it with water, watching the blue-gray smoke rise to the ceiling in long and curly swirls.

I return to my bed and position the candle on the night table, Drea's initials facing toward me. Then I grab a black pen from the drawer and draw a capital G across my palm— G for grandmother, so I will dream of her tonight, so I will dream of nothing else.

I crawl inside the covers and watch the candle burn the letters away, the capital D in Drea's initials already half gone.

Then I close my eyes and brace myself for sleep.

Two

I sit across from my grandmother at the kitchen table, snarfing down one of her famous grilled egg sandwiches and a stale bag of potato chips. I watch as her hands curl around the English muffin, and admire the amethyst ring on her fourth finger—a chunky violet stone that all but reaches her knuckle.

"Here." She notices me looking at it and tries to pry it off her finger. No go. She moves over to the sink and douses her hands in soap and water to lubricate the skin.

"It's okay, Grandma. You don't have to."

"I want to," she says, finally slipping it off and handing it to me. "Try it on."

I do; it's a perfect fit.

"It's your ring. I bought that for you when you were born. I've just been keeping it for you, until I thought you were old enough. Look at the initials inside."

I take it off and peek—the letters *S. A. B.* engraved in the gold. Stacey Ann Brown.

"It's beautiful," I say, handing it back to her.

"No," she says. "I want you to have it. I think it's time. Plus it fits your finger better than mine."

I slip it back on and kiss her cheek. "Thanks, Gram." I excuse myself from the table to go outside for some air. It's already nighttime, the sky an inky black canvas dotted with tiny dabs of light. A long, cloudlike puff of air smokes though my lips, and my teeth begin to chatter.

I can hear someone crying beyond the yard. I start walking toward the sound, and soon I'm past the fence, into the woods. With each step the crying gets louder, more insistent. "Drea?" I call. "Is that you?" It sounds just like her. I can just imagine her getting in another fight with Chad and trying to come and find me at Gram's.

Arms outstretched, I run in the direction of the whimpering. But then I have to stop. There's a singeing pain right below my stomach. I place my hands over my belly and breathe in and out. I have to pee.

I glance back in the direction of the house, but can't seem to see it now with the layering of trees and brush. Everywhere it's black. Even the dabs of light that I saw before are now painted over with dark branches.

A stick breaks from somewhere behind me. Then another. "Drea?"

I hold between my legs and hobble as best I can toward that faraway voice, dodging branches and brush with my one outstretched hand. I can feel the ground turn to mush beneath my feet. It slows me down until I stop altogether, try to catch my breath.

I can still hear Drea's voice, but it's farther away now, deeper into the forest. I strain to hear something else, anything that might tell me if I'm still being followed. But there's only the wind, combing through the frail, November leaves, whistling in my ear.

I take a small step and feel the ground get deeper, swallowing up my foot in a bottomless pit of heavy muck. More sticks break behind me.

I try to step out of the mud, to get out, but when I pull up my foot, my sneaker is gone.

Pain sears my stomach. I struggle to get away; I grab hold of a tree limb for support but end up slipping, landing down against my butt, the muck seeping in through my pants.

I count to twelve—the one-Mississippi, two-Mississippi method—and jam my thighs together, but it will only be minutes before I wet myself.

"Stacey," whispers a male voice from somewhere in the darkness.

I close my eyes and bury my head into my legs. Drea's faraway crying turns into a wail. She's calling me now, by name.

"You can't hide, Stacey," he breathes.

I can't give up. I search the ground for a rock or stick to protect myself. I find a rock. It isn't very big, but it has a nice, rough edge.

I arch my neck back to look up at the sky, knowing that the North Star will guide my way. I squint and blink hard to find it, but it's useless. Any trace of light is hidden beyond the treetops.

I crawl free of the mud completely, wrestle myself up, clench the rock into my palm, and trek for several seconds with my arms outstretched, brush scratching at my face like claws, until I reach a circular clearing. I look up to where the treetops have parted and can make out the sliver of the moon, approaching first quarter.

A rustling in the bushes distracts my attention. I look over, blink a few times, and see a man's figure standing between two trees a few feet in front of me. He doesn't move and neither do I, just extends his arm, as if to show me what he's holding. It's a bouquet of some sort.

I strain my eyes to see, using the moon as my light. And then it becomes clear to me—the size, the color, the way the petals fall open like a bell. They're lilies.

I know what lilies mean.

I run as fast as I can, my feet like a pair of mismatched ice skates over leaves and sticks.

Then I stop, clench my eyes, hear a full-fledged wail tear out of my throat. My one bare foot. I reach down to feel it—a narrow branch, stabbed into my arch as far in as it will go. I bite down on the skin of my thumb for several seconds, until I can swallow down some of the pain. I can't stay here. I need to get away. I have to be quick. I go to pull the stick out, but the throb in my stomach won't let me bend.

I clench my teeth, marry my thighs, and pray for all of it to go away. I lick my lips and squeeze my legs tighter. *Tighter*.

But it isn't enough. The warmth swells between my thighs. The front of my pants fills with dampness. I squeeze my legs to hold the water in place so he won't hear me, but my muscles ache from the effort. I feel my face tense, my eyes fill up. I can't hold it. The trickling leaks through my thighs, makes a pattering sound on the leaves beneath me.

"Stacey," he breathes, "I know your secret." The voice is slow and thick, the breath so close to the back of my neck that I reach back to swat it.

I open my mouth to scream but my throat is clogged, filled with dirt. It's everywhere. Up my nostrils. In my eyes. I grip around my throat to keep from choking, and realize the rock is still clenched in my palm. I dig my nails into its jagged ridges and throw it. Hard.

Crash. The sound of broken glass fills my senses. And when the lights come on I'm sitting up.

Three

"Stacey!" Drea shouts. She's flung herself out of bed to click on the light. "Are you all right?"

I hold my neck and allow myself to breathe, my throat no longer constricted with dirt. The window in front of our beds is broken, the glass shards strewn in chunky, jagged pieces all over the floor.

I look at Drea. She's sitting at the side of my bed now, looking at me for some answer, some explanation.

But how can I give her one when I don't even have a clue myself?

"Yeah, I'm fine," I say, gathering the covers around my waist, keeping my legs tucked together.

"You keep getting them, huh?"

It's no secret that I've been having this recurring nightmare ever since the start of school, but it is a secret that I've been wetting the bed because of it.

"Let's just hope it didn't wake up Madame Discharge."

Madame Discharge is the dorm's nickname for Ms. LaCharge, the resident director, because whenever she walks you can hear this faint squish sound in her pants, and she always smells like wet dog. Who am I to make fun, though? I spend all my extra money on incense and floral extracts to cover up my own little problem.

"What did you throw?" Drea asks.

I look over at the side of my bed. The blue candle with her carved initials only half-burned, down as far as the letter O. No wonder the spell didn't work the way it was supposed to.

"It must have been my crystal cluster rock," I say, noticing its vacant place by the lamp.

"I hope it didn't break."

"Crystal's stronger than glass," I say. "I'll look for it in the morning."

I'm relieved when Drea gets up from my bed to inspect the damage. I pluck the extra knitted afghan from the foot of my bed and spread it over my legs and middle, wondering if the lingering fumes of incense and candle are enough to cover up the nightmarish ones I have brewing beneath the covers.

"This should work." Drea pulls one of Chad's old hockey jerseys from her dresser. I wonder why she still has it; they haven't dated since last year. But since she's only using it for domestic repairs, I suppose I shouldn't be too jealous.

"What are you doing?" I ask.

"Just watch." She grabs a handful of hot roller clips from her vanity table and slips into her leopard-print clogs, the ones with the four-inch platform heels. "And you said I'd never find the perfect occasion to wear these." She clunks her way over to the window and pulls the orangy curtains closed. There's still about a six-inch gap left in between them. "This is what you get for a twenty-grand-a-year boarding school: cheap glass and tacky curtains that don't fit. You know they have Jacuzzis in some of the dorms at Fryer School? If I wasn't already a junior, I'd probably transfer." A gust of wind enters the room, causing a stream of English lit notes to fly off the dresser. "Could you get those?" she asks.

But I pretend not to hear, burying my nose into the capital G inked in my palm, thinking how my spell didn't work. I love Drea like a sister, but I don't want to dream about her anymore. Don't want to know the future before it happens.

Don't want to relive what happened three years ago.

I peek up at the watercolor picture on the wall. Me and Maura, the little girl I used to baby-sit, sitting together on a wooden porch swing.

"What do you think?" Drea asks, referring to the window, her patchwork. She's covered the hole completely by clipping Chad's hockey jersey across the width of both curtains, his number zero staring down at me like some subliminal message.

I give her the okay sign.

"Hopefully that will keep the cold out, but I'd bundle up for tonight. Who knows, maybe I'll give Chad a call. He could keep me warm." She raises her eyebrows and smiles.

I wonder if she knows how I feel about him, if she just drops these little bombs to drive me crazy.

"Tell you what," she says, "you clean up the glass and I'll charge the repairs tomorrow. I'm sure we can get someone in to replace it. Especially if we complain to security." She grabs her purse and begins combing through its contents. It's a designer brand, bought in Florence during her summer vacation—two-tone brown with tiny capital Fs printed all over the surface. She pulls out a matching F-printed wallet and slides a couple of dollars between her fingers. "I'm going down to the lobby to stock up on Diet Cokes. Wanna come?"

"No, thanks. I'll stay and clean up the glass."

She shrugs and turns on her platform heels. I watch her leave before creeping out of bed. The cotton fabric of my sweatpants clings between and at the back of my thighs in a warm and sopping wedge. The bed sheets, as well, are drenched, a bitter scent rising up from the puddle in the center. As icky as this whole scene is, I'm becoming more and more accustomed to it, the way I imagine mothers become accustomed to changing dirty diapers. Still, I have never had this problem before, even as a child. And what makes it worse is that I can't bear telling anyone, not even Drea.

I scurry through my disarrayed dresser drawers in search of another pair of blue sweatpants. I pull out a pair of dark jeans, a black sweatshirt, two pairs of corduroys, and a wool sweater before finally finding a pair. Only they're gray. Hopefully Drea won't notice.

I peel the sweatpants down my legs and kick them under my bed. The reflection of myself in the full-length mirror at the back of the door startles me—blanched skin dotted with eyes, nose, and mouth. A bit more blemished than my usual clear complexion. Brown eyes with red, wiry veins running through. Hair that hangs in dark clumps around my shoulders; hair that used to have body and luster, and be the envy of all my friends.

I turn sideways and my gaze travels down my body, noting my smallish waist—and the butt that's started to bubble out. Legs, nowhere near as shapely as they were this summer in my blue cut-off shorts. I wonder how long it's been since I looked in the mirror, when all these changes happened.

But I already know. I felt and looked so much better before I came back to school, before I started having these nightmares.

I wipe up my legs as best I can with a damp facecloth, yank on the pair of gray sweatpants, and glance over at the shoe rack in the corner of the room. Staring up from it is the pair of yellow sneakers I'm wearing in my nightmare. Each shoe has a thick, wooden bead threaded through the bottom lace. And embedded on the bead is the insignia for neutrality, two halves of the moon joined together by a line. They're my favorite sneakers, but I haven't worn them since the beginning of the year—because of my nightmares.

I slide open my night table drawer and pluck out a musk-scented incense cone and a bottle of lavender. The cone is about as tall as my thumb and carries a boylike scent when burned. I spill a few droplets of the oil onto my finger before wetting around the circumference of the cone. The combined scents are just enough to cover up the eau de toilette I've been creating since the beginning of school, and luckily Madame Discharge doesn't complain.

I know I need to hurry. Drea will be back any minute. I squat down beside my bed and grab a handful of plastic shopping bags. I've been making a habit out of taking a couple extra from the grocery store each time I go; now I have a whole stash.

I rip the soiled sheets from the bed, revealing the plastic bags I've placed underneath as a lining to protect the mattress. They're wet. I roll them up as best I can, stuff them under my night table, and then scurry to lay a few fresh ones down. The clean fitted sheet is a bit more difficult. I wrestle the first corner on, manage the opposite corner, try for the third, but then the first corner snaps back.

"Have another accident?" Drea is standing at the door, her arms full of Diet Cokes and chocolate bars from the lobby machines. "I hate it when that happens." She nods toward the bed sheets and I feel my face freeze.

"The hardest part is getting out the blood," she continues. "Usually I just send them to the cleaners. Is that why you changed?"

I nod.

"Ode to the joys of being a woman."

Relief. She doesn't know.

While Drea arranges her newly acquired lobby treats in an already crammed mini-fridge, I kick the soiled bedsheets underneath my bed and finish muzzling the clean one over all four corners of the mattress.

"Decided to burn some incense, I smell," she says. "You've been burning a lot of that stuff lately."

I ignore the comment and walk barefoot over to the broken glass. I begin sweeping it up using a brush that hasn't touched my hair in days and my math notebook, feeling a tinge of self-pride that I'm finally putting both to good use.

I walk the clump over to the wastebasket, but then stop, mid-dump. I snatch my eyes shut. Clench my teeth together. Hear a catlike cry whine out my throat. The sting shoots up my leg, up my spine, and forks into my shoulders and neck.

I missed a piece of glass. I lift my foot and turn it upward to look. The diamond-shaped chunk is still sticking out.

"I'll call the health center," Drea says. "Do you need an ambulance?"

"No. I think I can get it." I hobble over to my bed for a better look. I can see where the piece entered. A clean, sideways slit. I take a deep breath, grab the point that sticks out, and pluck the glass from my foot in one quick movement. A bright red piece, still dripping.

"Eauuw!" Drea dives headfirst into her bed, drowning her face into the sea of pink paisleys patterned across the comforter.

"I need you to go into my spell drawer," I tell her. "I need you to get me a potato."

"A potato?" Drea peeks out from the bed ruffle.

"Please."

She diverts her eyes toward the ceiling as she makes her way past me and into the bottom drawer of my dresser. She plucks out a hearty Idaho Gold.

"Cut it in half. There should be a plastic knife on the silver tray in there."

"Should I be worried?" she asks.

"Only if you don't hurry up."

Drea slices the raw potato in half and hands it to me. I press the damp, white center against the flesh and hold it there for many moments to clot the bleeding, an old family remedy even my mother uses. I top the cut off with a few drops of lemon juice and then bandage it up with some tape from the first-aid kit.

"Are you sure you're going to be all right?" she asks.

"I'm fine. Are *you* all right?"

"Actually I feel a little faint," she says. "Let me call the health center."

"For you or for me?" I joke. "It's two in the morning. It'll be fine for a few hours." I climb into bed and drag the covers up from the floor. "You know what's weird, though?"

"More weird than you and your potato?"

"Ha ha." I grab the half-burned candle with Drea's initials and stuff it into my night table drawer. "I cut my foot in my nightmare too."

"Hmm," she says. "That *is* weird. But sometimes nightmares come true."

I hesitate, wanting to say something, but don't. Even though I know I have to tell her soon. I have to tell someone.

four

It's 4:30 in the morning when the phone rings in our room. I'm up anyway, paging through back issues of *Teen People* for about the kagillionth time, trying to take my mind off those lilies in my nightmare.

I thankfully pause from last December's horoscope, the Taurean blurb reminding me how unsuccessful my love life has been, and nab the phone. "Hello?"

"Is Drea there?" An unfamiliar boy voice—lazy, muffled, distant.

I glance over at her. "She's sleeping," I say.

"Wake her."

"Um . . . no. But I'll have her call you at some normal time. You know, when people aren't sleeping? Can I ask who's calling?"

"A friend."

"Can you be more specific?"

But instead of answering, he hangs up. And so do I.

"Who was that?" Drea grogs.

"Some guy who wanted to talk to you," I say. "But he wouldn't give me his name."

Drea smiles.

"You know who it is?" I ask.

"Maybe," she says.

"Who?"

"Just some guy I've been talking to."

The phone rings again. I pick it up. "Hello?"

This time it's quiet on the other end. "Hello?" I repeat.

"Give it to me," Drea says.

I hand it to her and she turns away, cuddling up into a ball and talking in a whisper, so I can't hear her.

Maybe Chad's available after all.

I look over at his jersey, tacked up over the broken window, and imagine him wearing it—the sleeves scrunched up toward the elbow, a snug fit across the shoulders. I suddenly have the urge to go up, press my nose into the fabric, and lose myself in pheromonal bliss. But I know Drea would get all pissy on me if I even ventured a toe within a three-foot radius of the relic.

After several minutes of a whisper-filled conversation, Drea hangs up, and I'm still gawking at the jersey. "So who is this guy?" I ask.

"Nobody," she giggles.

"What do you mean, 'nobody'?"

"I mean, I don't want to talk about it right now," she says.

"Why? What's the big deal?"

"Let's end it, okay? It's no big deal."

"Fine," I say, paging past a string of shampoo ads in the magazine. I have no idea why she's getting all secretive on me.

"Chad's jersey really came in handy," she says, changing the subject.

"How come you still have it?"

"I don't know." She twirls a strand of hair around her finger and brings it up to her lip, mustache-style. "It's comfy and it still smells like him—the cuddly cologne he wears, the way his skin smells after a shower."

"Do you think you guys will get back together?" I ask.

"Naturally. We're so the same about everything. It's just a matter of time."

I squish down into my covers and try to conjure up his scent. The day we scarfed down mouthfuls of cherry pie at Hillcrest's homecoming pie-eating contest. The afternoon we spent searching for pinecones—an environmental science project—or cleaning up the campus for Earth Day. The time we almost kissed . . . and then did. But somehow, for some reason, even though the blood quakes through my veins just thinking about all these things, I can't remember how he smelled—the sexy, steamy scent that Drea is talking about.

There's a knock on the door. "Anybody order room service?"

It's Amber, our friend from upstairs. I hobble over to the door, my foot still stinging from the glass cut, and let her in.

"I totally couldn't sleep," she says, pushing past me. "And then I was walking by, heard you gals chattering away, and I figured I'd join you."

"Lucky us," Drea says.

"Oh my god." Amber folds her arms in front. "It's so totally freezing in here."

"We had an accident." Drea points toward the window.

"Bummer." Amber glances at the jersey-patch-up job for about half a second.

"Amber, it's 4:40 A.M.," I say. "Why are you up?"

"Hunger. You girls got anything to eat? I'm *so* starving." She boogie-dances over to Drea's mini-fridge, the pink and green shoes patterned across her woolly pajamas hopping along with her. She makes a "yuck" face at the selection inside—tongue slightly curled, sticking out to the side, one eye squinting, the other rolled upward—but then plucks out a granola bar. "So, why are *you* gals up?"

"We're up," I begin, "because some weird guy called Drea, but she won't talk about it."

"Who was it?" Amber asks.

"Just some guy," Drea says.

"Come on, Dray, you can do so much better than that," Amber says. "Info please."

"There is no info. It's just some guy I've been talking to. That's it."

"So, Chad's history?" Amber asks, winding one of her tiny orange pigtails around a periwinkle-blue nail-polished finger.

"Never history."

I reach for my school bag, slumped on the floor beside my bed, and pluck a deck of cards from the side compartment.

"Oh, Stacey," Amber begins, "tell me you're going to do a love spell. I'm so in. It's been a while, if you know what I mean."

"Oh, please," Drea says.

"Have some fun, will you? You're sixteen years old, in the prime of your life, at a coed boarding school with a boy to girl ratio of four to one. Advantage-in, if you know what I mean."

"For your information, I have lots of fun," Drea says.

"I know. I read it on the wall in the boys' bathroom."

"What were *you* doing in the boys' bathroom?" I ask.

"Writing stuff about myself. Gotta let the boys know I'm still in circulation."

"Maybe you'd have more luck if you took out a billboard ad on Route 128," Drea says. "What's it been, like, a year since you had a date?"

Amber sticks her tongue out at Drea, revealing a mouth-full of granola. "Six months, for your information. Almost as long as you and Chad have been broken up. God, you two were a lifetime ago."

"Eat your granola," Drea says.

"Takes more than granola to keep these lips shut," Amber says. "Listen, if you're not doing a love spell, I'm outta here. I've got toes to paint."

I peer down at her toenails, the pink and blue smiley faces with missing eyes and half-worn-off smiles. She ends up borrowing a bottle of nail polish remover from my desk and then raiding Drea's fridge for a Snickers bar and two cans of Diet Coke before leaving.

Meanwhile, since I'm pretty sure I won't be getting any more sleep tonight, and since the cards are already shuffled, when Drea asks for a reading, I *should*, but I don't, refuse.

We sit cross-legged on my bed, the cards in between us and thick, purple candles lit on both night tables. The rule-book says we aren't supposed to light candles or incense in the dorms, but nobody really pays attention to the rule-book anyway. Plus, Madame Discharge is usually too busy living vicariously through the contestants on *Blind Date*, blasting from her portable TV in the lobby, to even notice.

"Cut the deck into three piles," I say, "and make a wish before you make the third pile."

"Why the purple candles?" she asks.

"To help give us insight." I look down at my amethyst ring, remembering how I dreamed about it, remembering how my grandmother gave it to me when I was twelve, just before she passed away.

Drea makes her piles and I take seven cards from each to make one stack. "To your self," I say, placing the first card facedown. "To your family," I say, setting the second down next to it. I lay four more cards facedown and say their categories: "To your wish. What you expect. What you don't expect. What's sure to come true."

"Why don't you just use Tarot cards?" Drea asks.

"Because they're not as true. My grandmother taught me to read playing cards, just like her great-aunt taught her. The *real* way."

I lay the remaining cards down atop the others, creating piles of three and four. There are two cards left over, which I place to the side. "These are your surprise cards."

I turn the wish pile over to reveal a Nine of Spades, a Jack of Hearts, a Two of Clubs, and a Three of Spades, and feel the corners of my mouth turn down.

"What's wrong?"

"You made a wish about Chad."

"How can you tell?"

I point to the Jack of Hearts. "A fair-haired young man next to the Nine of Spades."

"What's a Nine of Spades mean?"

"Disappointment. The Two of Clubs tells me he's going to ask you out somewhere. But then he's going to disappoint you at the last minute."

"And the Three of Spades?"

"The Three of Spades is for tears."

"There's a surprise."

I place the wish pile to the side, facedown. "Do you want me to keep going?"

She nods.

I pick up the what-you-don't-expect pile and spread the three cards out to reveal an Ace of Clubs, a Five of Clubs, and an Ace of Spades.

I feel my face freeze up.

"What?"

"Nothing," I say, turning the cards over.

"If it doesn't mean anything, then tell me."

"Be careful, all right?"

"Be careful of what?"

But I can't answer. Can't say the words, like that will make them true.

Drea looks away to avoid eye contact—the way she always does when she doesn't get her way. "Fine, forget it," she says. "Don't tell me. I don't have time for games."

I focus a moment on the candle flame, following a tear of wax as it drips down the side. I don't know what to say, how to tell her, or if I should.

I peel the three cards back over and spread them out with my fingers. I swallow hard, try to think up something quick that will sound convincing. But instead I say, "Be careful you don't say something you might regret."

The expression on her face curls into a question mark. "*What?*"

"You know, watch what you say." My voice cracks.

"*'Watch what I say?'* Are you *serious*?"

"You may get into an argument with someone over it. Someone close to you."

"I do that anyway," she says. "Wow, Stace. You're a real mystic. You should open up your own shop and start charging people." She swings her legs off the side of the bed. "I have e-mail to check."

I hate having to lie, but it's better than telling her the truth. Even I don't want to face it. I collect the cards, but hold Drea's what-you-don't-expect pile aside.

"Why did Chad send me *this*?" Drea turns from her computer.

"What is it?"

"Some weird link about nursery rhymes. It's 'The House that Jack Built.'"

I join her to look. A computer-animated man in overalls and a tool belt moves around in a sort of computerized gait, laying down long slats of wood in the form of a house. In a matter of seconds, the construction is complete and the man has begun painting the exterior a creamy beige color.

"This is different," Drea says.

When the painting is done, a pearly white cat pounces down from a window ledge. It chases a rat across the front porch. The man wipes a stream of sweat from his brow and hammers up the finishing touch: a bright gold Welcome sign for the front door.

Drea clicks on it. A grandma-looking woman, wearing a long peach dress and a frilly apron, comes out on the front porch. She reaches into the pocket of her apron for a thin red book labeled Nursery Rhymes.

"This is the house that Jack built," the grandma-looking woman begins. "This is the rat that ate the malt that lay in the house that Jack built."

"Someone has a weird idea of humor," I say.

The wiry voice continues, "This is the cat that killed the rat that ate the malt that lay in the house that Jack built."

"Chad's such a weirdo," Drea laughs. "I was telling him the other day that I've been having trouble sleeping. I guess this is his idea of a bedtime story. You know, to lull me to sleep. He's so sweet." She clicks the page closed and checks her other messages. "Something from Donovan," she says, reading from the screen. "He's not going to be in health class, so can he borrow my notes." She types back a quick reply and sends it off.

"You know that's just an excuse," I say, moving back toward the bed. "He's probably missing class just so he *can* borrow your notes. Like health notes are even important."

Drea smiles; she knows it's true. "Nothing else from Chad," she sighs.

"Don't you think 'The House that Jack Built' is enough for one night?"

"I guess. I guess I just kind of miss the way he used to e-mail me good night." She flops back onto her bed and crawls under the covers. "Good night," she says.

"Good morning, you mean." I place Drea's cards into the night table drawer and roll the covers up over my shoulders. We still have another hour and a half before the alarm goes off. An hour and a half that I will spend staring up at the ceiling, thinking of Drea's card reading and of what I didn't—couldn't—say.

There is *no way* I'm going to fall asleep now.

five

D-period French. I slide down into my chair, sink my teeth into the pencil eraser, and flip through the four pages of the test. The subjunctive of *pouvoir*? The conditional past of *aller*? Is Madame LeSnore serious? She said this was going to be easy.

The room is church-silent as the traitor herself prances up and down the rows doing a final cheat-check, probably giggling on the inside at the sight of my sweaty face, twisted up in utter confusion. As she makes her way to the other side of the room, PJ, who sits beside me, and Amber, two chairs up, snicker silently back and forth about the shimmery blue tint Madame's sporting in her hair today. A definite Clairol emergency. Though I'm not sure why PJ thinks it's funny. He dyes his hair spikes more often than a chameleon changes color. Today he's settled on camouflage swirls to match his nail polish.

"Ten minutes left," Madame Lenore announces. "Stacey, stop daydreaming."

I blink my stare away from the ugly clay planter on her desk—a gift, she told us, from a former student *who appreciated the values of discipline and hard work*. Translation: a royal kiss-up.

PJ slides his test toward the end of the desk and then tilts it up in my direction. But all I can make out are the miniature doodles of comic-book characters playing cards and eating cheeseburgers that he's drawn in the corners.

"Your own work, please," Madame snaps. I bite the eraser completely off the end of the pencil and feel it wedge itself in my throat. A reflex shot: the soiled red nubby shoots out my mouth and into Veronica Leeman's bullet-proof hair. I'm all prepared to mouth out an apology, but with all that hair spray and gel, she doesn't even notice.

PJ rocks back and forth in silent laughter, his hands gripping over his stomach. "You rock," he mouths. I'm thinking Veronica senses the mockery because she turns around and gives him the finger.

I, on the other hand, am too tired to laugh. I need sleep more than this test. Besides, even attempting to fill in any of these blanks is a waste of fine pencil lead. I'll be begging Madame after class for a retake anyway. Why waste breath *and* school supplies?

I suddenly feel my eyes begin to droop closed and am literally fighting my head from bobbing back. I scrunch down a bit farther in my seat, hoping the back of the chair will help keep me propped, looking alert.

PJ's still laughing, audibly now. His mouth is arched wide open and his green, candy-dyed tongue is wriggling out his mouth like an angry snake. He pounds his fist down on the desk in hysterics, but no one seems to be paying any attention. No one even looks.

I don't have time to obsess on the subject of classroom injustice because suddenly . . . I have to pee. *Bad!* I place my hands over my stomach, cross my legs, and feel a droplet of sweat trickle down my forehead. I raise my hand to be excused, but Madame only laughs at me. She takes her seat at the front of the room and begins to correct my test, even though I haven't turned it in yet, even though it's still sitting on my desk, staring blankly up at me. This seemingly obvious setback doesn't seem to set her back from correcting it, however, because the next thing I know she's holding it up for everyone to see: a giant red *F* printed on the top.

PJ's mouth fills with even more laughter when he sees it, and his snakelike tongue writhes and twists out his mouth, trying to break free. Madame folds the test into a paper airplane and launches it at me. The plane circles the room a few times, but then lands in the center of my desk. I open up the folds and blink at the mass of words written in large, red, block letters across the paper: YOU KILLED MAURA AND DREA WILL BE NEXT.

"No, I didn't!" I scream. "I didn't kill her!" My shriek wakes me up and everyone's just . . . staring. It takes me a second to put it all together, that somehow I nodded off to sleep, right here, in the middle of class.

I look down at my test. It's still blank, still asking me for the subjunctive and conditional tenses. PJ reaches out his clunky, braceleted hand to my forearm, but even that startles me.

"Stacey?" Madame says. She stands up from her desk and looks me over, as though expecting to find some physical defect.

I have no idea what to say. A sprinkling of giggles shoots out from the front corner of the room.

"Students, please continue working," Madame says. "Stacey, are you all right?"

I nod.

More laughter, now from Veronica Leeman and her snotty friends.

"I hope this wasn't some idea of a joke." Madame looks at them and then at me.

I shake my head.

"Why don't you hand in your test and go to the office. *Now.*"

The legs on my chair scrape against the linoleum floor as I slide myself back from the desk. I want to slither away as slyly as PJ's tongue, but I can't. I need to hurry or I won't make it to the bathroom in time. All eyes in the class, except for Amber's and PJ's, reluctantly turn back to their meaningless French tenses. I walk to the front of the room and hand my blank test to Madame. She doesn't say anything else and I can't. I can only walk out of the room and resolve to stop whatever is going to happen. I have to save Drea and put Maura to rest in my mind forever.

Six

Dinner tonight looks gross. But since I skipped lunch after French class, mortified about what happened, I'm prepared to eat almost anything. I pluck one of the lemon-yellow trays from the stack, clank a handful of utensils on top, and peer over the row of heads in line to try to decipher what the gray mush being shoveled onto the plates is. Shepherd's Pie: bits of fatty scrambled hamburger in a mix of fake, waxy mashed potatoes and sweet, runny corn. *So* yucky.

Veronica Leeman stands ahead of me in line. I check her hair for my pencil eraser, but can't seem to locate it in all that mass. Darn. She notices I'm behind her and looks down at me as though I'm a squashed bug.

Veronica Leeman is one of the few people in this world I enjoy hating. Freshman year she organized a book drop in the middle of Algebra. At exactly 12:01, everyone except her and her three clone friends dropped their books. She and her friends just sat at their desks, hands folded, heads cocked to the side, feigning confusion. The result: the rest of the class, me included, got a week's worth of mind-deadening detention with Mr. Milano, the biology teacher, who decided it would do us some good to listen to him lecture for hours about his dissertation research—the mating habits of reptiles.

The line moves forward, and me and Veronica are next. I watch as she grimaces over the selection of food. "Shepherd's Pie?" cafeteria-lady asks, an ice-cream scooper full of the chunky mixture aimed over Veronica's plate in plop position.

"Heinous," Veronica says, waving her red acrylic nails like a stop signal. "Who eats this stuff?"

"You do, now," cafeteria-lady says.

"I don't think so. I'm a vegetarian."

The woman plops some onto Veronica's plate. "Try it."

"Didn't you hear me? I'm a vegetarian. Veg-i-tar-i-an. I don't eat an-i-mals. Which word don't you understand?"

Cafeteria-lady smacks the ceramic plate back onto the counter and hands Veronica a cellophane-wrapped sandwich labeled TUNA.

"Since when is a fish not an animal? Don't you have any salad?"

"Just corn and mashed potatoes."

"Fine. I'll have that."

A splash of corn juice hits Veronica's cheek as cafeteria-lady shakes the yellow glob onto the plate with the scooper. So perfect.

"Thanks a lot." Veronica clanks the plate onto her tray and moves away.

I take the rejected tuna sandwich and sit at a table in the corner of the cafeteria, where the kids in the drama club congregate. It isn't my usual spot, but I want some peace and quiet and know they'll be too engrossed in arguments over whether or not Hamlet really had it hard for his mom to care about my episode in French class. Plus, sitting here also gives me the opportunity to piece things together.

I consider the cards first. They say Chad is going to ask Drea out someplace but then cancel last minute, but that's really nothing new. They've *both* been active players in the game of date tag for as long as I've known them.

She also got the Ace of Clubs, which is for a letter she'll receive; the Five of Clubs, for a package. But the card that really freaks me out the most is the Ace of Spades, the death card, which landed smack dab in the middle of both.

The death card, just like the lilies.

I tear up my sandwich into tiny pieces, remembering how one Easter Gram went completely ballistic when a neighbor brought a bunch of lilies over for the table's centerpiece. She ended up chopping the flowers from the stems and cramming them all down the garbage disposal.

Then, the following day, she brought me to a garden shop and spent what seemed like hours teaching me about flowers and what they mean—like how lilies mean death.

The man in my dream was holding a whole bunch of them.

What about the smell of dirt? The scent was so potent in my nightmare; I can almost smell it now, just thinking about it.

"Hey, Stacey." Chad places his tray down opposite mine. It's loaded with his usual amount—three ham sandwiches, two bags of ripple chips, a two-pack of yellow frosted cupcakes, three cartons of milk, an apple, and a banana.

He doesn't normally sit with us in the cafeteria. Being the star goalie on Hillcrest's hockey team, he normally spends most of his time with teammates. I suspect he wants something.

"Hey, Stace," Drea says, sitting down next to him.

Amber and PJ join us, one sitting on each side of me. It's mourning silent, but I can still feel the laughter building up inside them, like a carbonated bottle about to blow.

"Okay," I say. "Let's hear it."

"Hear what?" PJ asks. "What's the matter, Stace? You look a little tired. Didn't you catch up on enough sleep in French class? Or were you too busy killing people?"

Laughter released—a carbonated explosion. PJ and Amber high-five one another over my head.

"Hysterical," I say. "So I haven't been sleeping great lately and dozed off during French. Can you blame me?"

"I really think you need to talk to someone, Stace," Drea says. "Maybe a sleep disorder therapist or something."

"And if that wasn't priceless enough," PJ begins, "seconds before she falls asleep, she goes all exorcist-chick on us and she spews out in Snotty Ronnie's hair."

"A pencil eraser," I correct. "And I spit it up; I didn't spew it out." Like it even makes a difference.

"Speaking of . . ." Amber motions to the table to our right. Veronica is sitting there with her friends, pointing toward PJ and me and making that high-pitched cackle she calls a laugh. She focuses on PJ, makes the L-for-loser sign with her fingers, and places it up to her forehead. Veronica's lemming-friends follow suit.

PJ focuses on his lunch, pretending it doesn't bother him.

"Are you *kidding*?" Amber asks. "Don't back down. Tell that bitch off. Stacey, do one of your spells on her. Make her get fat."

"Whatever spell I do comes back at me three times. I think I've gained enough this quarter."

"So right," Amber says, glancing down at my waist.

Amber can be such a bitch.

"She's not worth it." PJ pours a bit of orange soda into his milk—a daily ritual he calls delicious—and drinks in audible gulps. "I hate her, though. I wish she'd croak."

"You don't mean that," I say.

"How do you know?"

I guess I don't know. It's just weird hearing PJ talk that way about anyone. PJ, who refuses to swat at flies because of the karmic penalty, who got caught last year trying to free Mrs. Pinkerton's pet rabbit from its cage in the chemistry lab.

"Speaking of death," Amber begins, "dreaming about killing people in the middle of class is kind of freaky, don't you think, Stace?" She peels open her peanut butter sandwich and layers the inside with barbecue-flavored potato chips.

"Do you think it has something to do with those nightmares you've been having?" Drea scooches her chair in closer to Chad's.

"Nightmares?" PJ turns toward me. "I didn't know you've been having nightmares. That's so famous. Do tell."

"Was I not supposed to mention that?" Drea asks.

"Why not," Amber says. "Everybody knows Stacey can sometimes see shit about people in her dreams. I'm just waiting for her to see shit about me. Like when I should expect Brantley Witherall to give me a jingle."

"I think you've jingled enough this year," Drea says.

Amber lizard-flips her tongue out at Drea in retaliation, exposing a size seven barbell. "Maybe he's already called." She reaches into her Hello Kitty lunch box of a purse for her cell phone. She presses at the buttons, waiting for it to work.

"Let me guess," Drea says. "No charge."

"Why do I always forget?"

"Because your name is Amber." Drea forks a cubed tomato into her mouth. "Just put the phone away before we all get in trouble."

Ms. Amsler, our gym teacher, is in charge of dinner duty tonight, but luckily she's more interested in the slop cafeteria-lady is serving up to concern herself with cell phones or barbells.

I look down at my chips and see that I have arranged them on my tray in the shape of a heart. Completely mortified at my subconscious' perpetual desire to embarrass myself, I cover the chips up with what's left of my sandwich and peek at Chad to make sure he hasn't noticed.

He's looking straight at me, his off-centered smile curling to the left. "So, what happens in these nightmares?" He flips the most perfect chunk of stray sandy-blond hair from in front of two equally perfect greenish-blue eyes.

"Well, it's not really clear yet," I swallow, my voice cracking on the word *really*. "There's this guy and he's sort of following me."

"Can you see his face?"

I shake my head. "I can hear his voice though; it's familiar, but I can't place it."

He leans in closer. "Maybe it just means you're running from something—or someone—who's close to you . . . and that you shouldn't be."

I focus into the refuge of my tuna, feeling my cheeks warm over, feeling a smile fight its way across my mouth. Is he really saying what I think he's saying or am I completely reading into it? I look back up and he's smiling too, like we're both caught in some weird, romantic-comedy sort of moment. Lucky for us we have Drea to zap us back to the reality of cafeteria food.

"You know, Chad," she begins, "that e-mail you sent me was so cute."

"What e-mail?" He grins.

"The nursery rhyme? 'The House that Jack Built'? *So* cute."

"I don't know what you're talking about."

"You don't have to be embarrassed," Drea says. "Stacey already saw it and I forwarded the link to Amber. Couldn't resist. *Too* cute."

I'm not even sure he's still listening to her. He unzips his backpack, plucks out his English notebook, and folds it open to some notes on *Beowulf.*

"Put that away." Drea snatches the notes away. "This isn't the library. Besides, so rude. It's lunch time and we're trying to have some intellectual conversation here."

"Looks like *you* picked the wrong table," Amber says.

Chad looks at me and smiles, like he's about to say something.

"Hi, Donovan," Drea squeals, as Chad's roommate, Hillcrest Hornets' prize hockey center, walks by. She props Lefty and Righty, her two cuppiest assets, onto the table.

Meanwhile, I'm still focusing on Chad, waiting for him to continue our conversation, hanging on by barely an eyelash because he's not even looking at me now. His attention has wandered to Drea, flirting with Donovan, stuffing her hands into the pockets of his blazer.

"I *know* you have gum for me." She glances at Chad, checking to make sure he's paying attention.

He is.

Donovan reaches into the inner pocket of his navy-blue uniform blazer and pulls out a pack of Juicy Fruit. He gives her a piece. "And one for later," she purrs. He gives her another.

Amber pokes her finger into her mouth, I'm-gonna-puke style. I nod my agreement.

Drea stuffs both pieces of gum into her mouth, crumples the wrappers into silver wads, and presses them into Donovan's palm. "Could you be a sweetie and dump these for me?" Without the slightest hesitation, he turns and walks the six or seven tables down to the trash can, slipping on a squashed grape in the process.

"*Such* a catch," Amber says, fluttering her eyelashes toward Drea.

Drea scowls. "Jealous that I have guys literally falling over me."

When Donovan returns to the table, Drea makes room for him on the seat beside her. "I missed you in health class this morning. Where were you?"

It's no secret that Donovan sweats Drea. She knows it. He knows she knows it. *Everybody* at Hillcrest knows it. As legend has it, Donovan has been sweating over Drea ever since the third grade, when they went to grammar school together, but she's just never given him a chance.

"I was working on some of my art," he says. "I got permission from Mr. Sears to miss the class."

"Got any pictures to show?" Amber asks. "I love looking at your work." She leans her chin against his shoulder and smiles at Drea.

Donovan pulls a mini-sketchbook from his back pocket and flashes us a charcoal drawing of a room, empty except for a cushy chair, a night table, and a door with no knob.

"Talk about no exits," Amber says. "*C'est très Existentialiste* of you."

"Like you even know what that means," Drea says.

"Are you kidding? Camus is my man. So deep. Such art."

"That's Sartre, you nitwit." Drea pushes Amber out of the way to get a closer look at the sketchbook. She snatches it out of Donovan's hands and begins flipping through the pictures.

"Wait—" Donovan moves to grab the sketchbook back, but Drea turns to avoid him.

"I want to see," she whines. She flips the pages over sketches of flowers, bowls full of fruit, a pair of glasses, and then stops at a picture of a girl who has an unmistakable resemblance to herself.

"Is this me?" Drea asks.

The sketch is done in bright violet charcoals. In it, the girl is huddled underneath an umbrella, wearing a short raincoat and an extra smear of shadowing under her eye, like she's crying.

"It's just doodling." Donovan takes the sketchbook back.

"It's from last week, isn't it? I recognize the raincoat."

"Why were you crying?" I ask.

"Parent stuff, what else?" Drea looks away, but then smiles at Donovan to break the tension. "You could have at least made me look happy. And look at my hair. Do you know what moisture-filled air does to hair, even under an umbrella?"

"I prefer drawing people exactly the way I see them. They're perfect just the way they are. Real, you know?"

"You are so not the hockey type," Amber says, extracting a floral pair of chopsticks from her lunch box.

"No, he's the *perfect* type. Creative, smart, *and* athletic." Drea links her arm with Donovan's. "Maybe you'd like to sketch me when I'm looking a bit . . . perkier."

"I've got some time now," Donovan says.

Drea smiles in Chad's direction, collects her tomato salad, and makes her grand exit with Donovan.

"Why does that always happen?" Amber stabs her chopsticks into the table.

"What?"

"She always gets the guy."

"I'm right here." PJ leans in for a kiss, but Amber jams a grape in his mouth.

"I thought you always said Donovan was a creep," I say.

"He is."

"Then why do you flirt with him?"

Amber shrugs, plucking out all the green grapes from her fruit salad with the chopsticks. I look over at Chad, who has fallen silent, his eyes locked on the image of Drea and Donovan walking away.

Seven

It's late when I get back to the room. I ended up spending a good chunk of the evening studying for the French test I'm hoping Madame LeSnore lets me retake. I've already decided I will apologize to her first thing in the morning, saying that I've been having some family problems back home. It isn't so far from the truth. My mother couldn't have been happier when September rolled around and I had to go back to school.

It's not that me and my mother don't get along. We just don't get along *well*. Sometimes I think it might have something to do with my dad. He passed away when I was just seven years old. You'd think that would bring my mother and me closer—leaving just the two of us to brave the world on our own, to keep his memory alive. But it hasn't. I wonder sometimes if it just pulled us further apart—like maybe my mother would have been happier as I was growing up if she had a partner, a soulmate, to raise me with. It's not like she's some modern-day Mommie Dearest or anything. Some of my friends over the years have said they'd kill to have such a cool mom like mine—a mother who still reads *Seventeen* and goes tanning and gets her acrylics filled. Who knows the names of all the boys in school because *my* friends dish to her about them—even more than they dish to me. The truth is we're just different. I'm more like my gram. That's why I miss her so much. And *that's* what irks my mother so much.

"Drea?" I fling my backpack to the floor and glance at Drea's side of the room—bed still made, last night's pajamas still in a heap at the foot of her bed. It doesn't look like she's been back here yet. I wonder if she's still with Donovan.

I squat down by the side of the bed and collect the soiled laundry underneath. I've learned that if you're quick to clean up the mess, it doesn't smell as much. But I've already left this stuff too long. You can see a cloudlike outline of golden brown on one of the sheets, and they smell like dirty diapers.

I squish everything inside a pillowcase filled with dirty school-uniform parts, grab the soiled plastic shopping bags from underneath my night table, and make the five-minute trek across the dorm parking lot to the washroom. I swing the door open, promptly dump the plastic bags into the trash, and flop the sack of dirty laundry onto one of the machines. I begin separating the lights from the colors and darks, the way the mom-looking women do on TV commercials for laundry detergent. That's when I notice a pink bra, stuck between a fold in the sheet and statically clung to Drea's lacy white handkerchief. I know the bra isn't mine, but I hold it up to my chest anyway. *Definitely* not mine. The cups stick out so confidently, it's almost as if they could get a date all by themselves.

I'm just about to deposit the bra into the machine when I feel the bra's vibrations. They come over me all of a sudden, like tiny pins of electrifying heat that charge through my arms and point down my fingers. I move the silky fabric between my fingers and the feeling deepens, like someone has taken hold of my skin, dug their claws right into the flesh.

I hold the bra up to my nose to sniff. It's the smell of fresh air mixed with dirt. The smell of my nightmare.

There's no doubting it. Drea's in trouble.

I fling the bra down and boot it as fast as I can back to the dorm, the throb at the bottom of my foot from the glass injury reminding me that I'm probably due for a bandage change.

"Drea!" I shout, bursting into our room.

She's standing in front of the window, a chocolate bar in her right hand and a scowl across her face. "Did you take it down?" she asks.

"What?"

"It's totally freezing in here. Why did you take it down?"

"Take what down?"

"Chad's hockey jersey!"

It takes me a few moments to put it all together. Her anger. The empty window. The missing jersey. "I didn't," I say, finally.

"Then what happened to it? Nothing just disappears."

"What are you saying? That I took it? Why would I do that?"

"You tell me. I saw the way you were looking at him in the cafeteria today. Don't deny it."

"Oh, and it wasn't *you* who went off with Donovan? Don't take it out on me if Chad didn't go running after you. He and I are just friends, Drea. That's it."

Drea studies my eyes, as though trying to decide whether or not to believe me. "I'm a shit, aren't I?"

"Yes," I say. "But I love you anyway." We share a smile and then Drea tears the foil wrapper farther down her candy bar and passes it to me for a bite—for her, a rare and generous offer, which tells me that she *really* feels like a shit. And that just makes me feel worse because I know I was kind of looking at Chad in that way.

"Maybe the jersey just fell outside," I say, changing the subject. I grab the window shade and pull a bit too hard, causing it to snap back and coil up at the top. There's a package outside, sitting on the brick window ledge. It's about the size of a ring box and wrapped in turquoise paper with a tiny red bow on top.

My heart wallops inside my chest. It's really happening, just as the cards predicted.

"A present!" Drea bursts, the anger quickly evaporating from her face. "I wonder if it's from Chad."

Part of me wants to leave it out on the window ledge and pretend like I never saw it. But it's too late now. I have to know if the cards are true.

I reach through the glass and pluck the box from the ledge. "We really need to get this window fixed. I'm not comfortable with people hanging around outside our room. We live on the ground floor, for god's sake; anyone could just break in."

"It wasn't just anyone," Drea corrects. "It was Chad. I'm so sure." She snatches the box out of my fingers and toys with the ribbon.

"Where were you tonight, anyway?" I ask.

"Wouldn't you like to know? You saw me leave the cafeteria with Donovan."

"You were with him all this time?"

"No, but I wanted Chad to think I was. I guess he did." She smiles at the present.

I keep my eyes focused on her fingers, fearful of what might happen. I see she's tempted to pull on the ribbon. "No!" I shout. "Don't!"

"Why?"

"Just don't." If the deathly thing is going to happen to *her*, it's safer if *I* open it. "I want to open it. I never get presents." I nab the box back and shake it softly. There's a tiny shift inside.

We perch ourselves on the end of the bed and inspect the package for a name tag. Only we can't find one.

"I don't understand it," Drea says. "Chad always attaches a card."

"Maybe he just forgot," I say. "Or maybe it's inside."

Drea continues to comb her fingers over the tiny package—under the bow, in the creases, and under the bottom flap.

"Maybe he doesn't want you to know it's from him," I say. But I know that isn't the truth either. This package isn't from Chad. This is the package I predicted in the card reading, and in some way it's linked with my nightmares.

"Fine," she says, giving up. "Go ahead."

I stare down at the package for several seconds, wondering if now is the right time to tell Drea the truth about the card reading.

"That's it!" she shouts. "This is ridiculous. I've waited long enough." She snatches it out of my fingers and tears off the top layer of paper.

"Wait!" I say, finally. "I lied!"

But it's too late. Drea has already ripped off the wrapping and bow.

"No!" I shout, tearing it out of her hands. "Don't!" I fling the package to the floor and stomp on it. Nothing happens. I kick it against the wall. Still nothing. I don't know whether to sing or be sick, but I'm completely overwhelmed with this enormous feeling of relief.

"What is *wrong* with you?" Drea asks. "Have you gone completely crazy?"

I look at her, at the droop of her mouth, the confusion on her face.

"I think you killed it," she says.

I pick up the crushed box, take in a long, deep breath, and with slightly jittery hands remove the cover. We look down at the contents. Tiny crumbs of tan mixed with chocolate brown. Drea dips her fingers into the box and tastes one of the pieces. "Chocolate chip cookie. Or at least it was one." She flicks the bits of cookie to the sides of the box, and underneath, finds a note the size of a fortune cookie message: "Be a smart cookie," she reads. "Join the culinary arts club."

She sticks her head out the window and looks to the left. "There's one on everybody's window ledge. Cute idea, huh?"

Maybe I *am* going crazy.

"You need to relax," she says. "Do you think one of them stole Chad's hockey jersey? Because if they did, I'm going to report them to campus police first thing in the morning." She takes another bite of her chocolate bar. "Hey, what did you say before about lying?"

"Nothing. I'm just tired." I pocket the cookie message and look out the broken window at the velvety night sky. There, in the peaceful whirring of the wind, I can almost hear my grandmother's voice, telling me to trust my insight, telling me that it's when we don't that tragedy occurs.

I know firsthand that's true.

I fold back onto the bed, close my eyes, and conjure up my warmest memory of Maura. It was all warm and balmy out that day, as though at any minute the cloud lining would unzip and rain would sprinkle down in feathers. Maura and I were sitting on the wooden porch swing at her house and I was showing her a magic trick. I shuffled the deck of cards and held them out in a fan. "Pick a card. Any card." Maura giggled and picked from the middle. "Now look at it, remember it, but don't tell me which one it is."

She nodded and smiled, her tongue peeking through the gap between her top and bottom teeth, red Kool-Aid stains around her mouth.

"Now put it back, wherever you want."

Maura placed the card to the left of the fan. I swallowed it up in the other cards and shuffled. "O magic, magic, do your trick," I said for her amusement. "Tell me true which card to pick." I flipped the cards, one by one, faceup on the swing, and tried to guess which card was hers. I slapped the Queen of Diamonds down and paused. I looked up at her and she giggled.

"Nope," she said.

I wiped the strawberry-tinted bangs from her eyes and flipped a few more cards. I stopped on the Ace of Hearts. "Is this the one?"

Maura started clapping. She wrapped her arms around my neck. The smell of her clothes, like popcorn and red licorice, reminded me that I had been way too lenient about afternoon snacks. "Can you teach me?" she asked.

"Sure I can teach you. But first you need to wash your face for dinner."

"Can I tell you a secret first?"

"Sure."

"I wish you were my sister."

"Me too," I said, squeezing her extra tight.

I open my eyes and glance over at Drea, brushing her hair in the mirror, getting in all one hundred strokes. And all I can think is how I never got that chance to show Maura how the trick worked.

"Drea," I say, "I lied to you about your card reading. And it's time you knew the truth."

Eight

"What do you mean, *you lied?*" Drea smacks her hairbrush down on the vanity table and swivels around in her seat to face me.

"I mean I wasn't completely honest about the outcome of your card reading. I'm sorry. It was stupid. I just didn't know how to tell you the truth."

"What *is* the truth?"

"Everything I said about Chad making a date with you and then breaking it is true, but the other stuff—"

The phone rings, interrupting me. Drea gets up to answer it. "Hello?" she says. "Yes, thanks for getting back to me. This is the second time I've had to call about our broken window. When can I expect someone to fix it?"

When I hear her mention Chad's jersey being missing, I turn away, figuring she's talking to campus police. I can't blame her for getting all huffy at me for lying—I'd be huffy too. I just hope it doesn't jeopardize her trust in me later on.

I lean back on my bed and take in a deep breath. And then I remember. My laundry. In the washroom. The pee-stained sheets. I consider walking back over there, but after the cards and lying and that stupid cookie gift, I decide my heart has absorbed enough shock for one night. I will set my alarm to vibration mode for 5 A.M. tomorrow morning, stash it under my pillow, and run over to the washroom before anyone is even awake.

Drea clicks the phone off, but then starts dialing again. Calling Chad, I presume.

Instead of dwelling over it, I decide to be productive. I get up and fish into the back of my closet for the family scrapbook. Heavy and cumbersome, it has torn and yellowing mismatched pages and burn marks in the corners. It's packed with all sorts of passed-down materials—home remedies, spells, bits of favorite poetry, even secret recipes, like my fifth cousin's coffee braids.

My grandmother gave the book to me two weeks before she passed away, and every time I use it I picture women, ages ago, in long apron-dresses, doing spells or reading magical poetry by candlelight. When I asked my gram how she got it, she told me that her great-aunt Ena gave it to her, and that I should pass it along to someone else one day, someone like me who has the gift.

I peel the book open to a half-crumpled page signed by my great-great-great aunt Ena. It's a home remedy to help cure night-blindness: raw fish liver for dinner. Gross, but it probably beats the cafeteria food. I page through the book a bit more. I want to do a dream spell tonight, one that waxes my nightmares to fullness instead of waning them away.

I don't use the book often, especially because Gram always said it wasn't good to rely on it, that spells or remedies come from within, and that we are the ones who give them meaning. But whenever I do use it, I love to look at the handwriting—places where the pen skipped and caused a tiny splash, or places where the ink bled. Those who had a tendency to slant the letters versus those who wrote all bubbly. I can almost imagine the personalities of these women just by looking at their names, the way they wrote them, and what they chose to contribute. It always leaves me with a magical sense of connection to my family, even to those I never met.

I have never performed this type of spell before, but if I want to change the future and save Drea, I need more clues.

I light a stick of lemongrass incense. Then I gather up the tools I need and lay them on my bed: a branch of rosemary, an empty pencil case, a bottle of lavender oil, and a yellow wax crayon. The pencil case is the baglike kind, lined inside, with a zipper at the top. Like my gram, I always keep potential spell items on hand. Even if I never find a use for some of the stuff, even if she always pledged that the most essential spell ingredients are in the heart, it's just one more way I can feel connected to her.

I reach inside the drawer for a candle, pausing at the blue one I used last night, Drea's initials—the half-burned *O*, the *E*, and the *S*—stare up at me. Her initials stand for Drea Olivia Eleanor Sutton, and have been the butt of jokes ever since I've known her. Guys say stuff like "Drea DOES it best" and "Drea DOES anything, anytime." At first I thought she was asking to get harassed. She has the initials stitched to practically everything she owns, for god's sake—her towels, stationery, sweaters, even on her school backpack. But then I realized, who were we to tell her to change? Drea's defiance is just one of the things I love about her.

"Shit," she says, slamming the phone down. "Chad isn't in his room. What am I supposed to think now?" She joins me on the bed and glances down at her chipped, French-manicured toes.

"I'm sorry for lying about the cards," I say. "But it was only because I was scared."

"Whatever, I'm too depressed to care about that now." She looks over the spell ingredients sitting between us.

"Well, you need to care because tonight this spell involves you." I pinch the lip of the clay pot and pass it three times through the incense smoke. Then I light the candle and place it on the night table. It's purple and white, the product of two parent candles melted together in a sort of wax communion.

"That's funky."

"It's symbolic," I explain. "The purple is for insight; the white is for magic. The union of the two symbolizes the union of the images I've been having in my dreams. Can you give me a blank page from your diary?"

"Why?"

"Because the pages hold your energy, even the blank ones. And this spell is for you."

She reaches into her night table drawer for the diary, thumbs to the back, and tears out a page. "What's this all about?"

"I told you we needed to talk."

The phone rings again. Drea springs to answer it. "Hello? Oh, hi." She turns away from me and resumes her conversation in a whisper.

I'm assuming she's talking to him again—the guy who called early this morning. And I know it should make me jump for joy, since it's not Chad she's talking to, but it doesn't. I have no idea who this guy is and it's not like Drea to keep her crushes a secret.

When she finally does hang up, she looks upset. She flops onto her bed, scrunches up her knees, and reaches for the medicinal bar of chocolate. I'm all ready to ask her about it, but the phone rings again. This time I answer it. "Hello?"

Silence.

"Give it to me," Drea says.

I shake my head. "Who is this?"

Still nothing. I hang up.

"It was probably for me," Drea says.

"If he wants to talk to you, why can't he just ask? Who is this guy? And why does he keep pranking us?"

There's a knock at the door. I get up slowly from the bed, pluck the baseball bat from behind the door, and curl my hand around the knob. "Who is it?" I demand.

"Who else would it be this late?" says the voice on the other side.

Amber. I can breathe again.

"What is wrong with you?" Drea asks.

I open the door.

Amber looks at the baseball bat positioned over my shoulder. "Trying out for the team? I'd rethink. Polyester stretch and cleats are so not a good look for you."

"Amber, have you been getting any pranks? Drea and I have been getting a lot of them lately."

"They're not pranks," Drea says.

"It's probably PJ," Amber says. "He likes to prank people. He used to prank me all the time while we were dating." She sprawls out on Drea's bed and kicks her legs back and forth. "Your bed is so incredibly comfortable compared to mine. Care to trade for tonight?"

"So you haven't been getting any?" I ask.

Amber shakes her head. "Did you star-six-nine them?"

Light dawns. I grab the phone and dial. "Blocked."

"Figures," Amber says. "PJ always star-six-sevens before he dials. Oldest trick in the book. PJ taught it to me. Maybe it is him. I'll ask him tomorrow in French class. Wanna do a love spell?"

I fish my hand into the trash and pluck out the mangled box with the cookie. "Did you get one of these cookie presents?"

"Some cookie," Amber says.

"It kind of had an accident," I say. "It was left on the window ledge."

"Sweet," Amber says. "I love secret admirers. Who's it for?"

I take the message from my pocket and hand it to her.

"I guess the culinary arts club doesn't want me to join," she says. "Who wouldn't want to taste these cookies?"

"Shall I start the list?" Drea yawns.

The phone rings again. Drea goes to grab it, but I get there first. "Hello. Hello? I know you're there."

"Give it to me," Drea says.

I shake my head and listen. I can hear someone breathing on the other end—thick, even breaths. And then he finally hangs up.

"Drea," I demand, clicking the phone off, "who is this guy?"

"I told you. He's just someone I've been talking to."

"What's his name?" I ask.

"I don't know," she says. "It's not important anyway."

"His name isn't important?"

"Names are just tags we put on to label ourselves," she says. "They don't mean anything."

"What are you talking about?"

"Forget it," she says. "I didn't think you'd understand."

"Does he go here?" Amber asks.

She shakes her head.

"Then how do you know him?"

"Well, not that it's any of your business," she says, "but he called here one night by accident, basically a wrong number, and we just started talking."

"Do you call *him*?" I ask.

"No. He says he can't give his number out."

"Why?"

"Hey, I'm not on trial here. Enough questions." Drea pulls the diary from her drawer to write.

"*So* not smart." Amber extracts a pack of cigarettes from the pocket of her pajamas, taps the box against her palm, and lights one with the candle flame. She sucks on the cigarette as though it's an asthma inhaler.

"Since when do *you* smoke?" I ask.

"Since I found an only half-used pack in the lobby."

"Well, if Madame Discharge smells that, we're all dead."

"I think it's airy enough in here, don't you?" Amber makes fish faces as she blows O-shaped puffs of smoke toward the broken window. "Besides, with that stuff you're burning, it smells like skunk piss in here."

I wave the tendrils of smoke from my face before moving over to the corner window, the one that isn't broken. It's black outside—just a few scattered stars in the distance. I make a wish on one of them, for peace and safety. The glass is chilly, like the room, and the heat of my breath forms a cloud. I draw a peace sign in the middle of it with my finger and then peer down through my print.

There's a man looking up at me from the lawn. It's hard to see too well in the darkness, but I can tell he's older, maybe forty or fifty-ish, and that he has sort of dark, wispy hair. He's wearing a pair of jeans, I think, and holding a large shopping bag. When he sees that I notice him, he looks away, toward the windows of the other rooms. "Guys, there's somebody out here spying on us."

"What?" Drea joins me at the window to look. "Maybe it's a janitor."

"Maybe we should call security," I say.

"And tell them what?" Amber says. "That one of the janitors is working outside? Big news flash. They'll have us committed."

"We already called them once tonight," Drea says.

"You guys are worse than a couple of old ladies." Amber bounces up and in between us to look. Her eyes widen. "Hel-looo, Big Boy," she says. "Not bad. Not bad at all. Eat your heart out, Brantley Witherall. Maybe there's hope for me yet."

"Are you kidding?" Drea says. "He's ancient."

"Yeah, well, times are tough." Amber combs her hands down the front of her pajama top, all sexylike, then flips the top up, revealing two lacy red demi-cups, her boobs oozing out the top.

"Amber!" Drea screeches, pulling her away from the glass. "What do you think you're doing?"

"Lighten up," Amber says. "See, it just goes to show you, don't laugh when Mom tells you to always wear good underwear."

"*Clean* underwear," Drea corrects.

I remain at the window, staring out at the man from behind the curtain. I can tell that he's tall, and from the movement of his body as he walks, searching the other windows, that he's also very strong. He peers in my direction and smiles, somehow able to see me. I panic and pull the shade down.

"You guys are just too paranoid," Amber says, chomping on Drea's candy bar. "There's enough security around here to keep god away."

"Easy for you to say," Drea says. "You don't live on the ground floor."

"Fine, you want me to call campus police?" Before Drea or I can answer, Amber is dialing. "Hi, Officer," she says. "I'm in Room 102 Macomber Center. Yeah, and there's this incredibly hot guy with pecks to die for and the tightest little ass outside our window. Now, he's probably a janitor, but we're not sure, so what do you suggest we do?" Amber dangles the phone away from her ear. "What do you know? He hung up on me. That's, like, so rude."

"I can't believe you just did that," I say. "They're never going to believe us now."

"Believe what?" she says.

"Look, Amber," I say, "Drea and I need to talk, and I need to do this spell while the moon is still in position."

"Don't let *me* stop you."

"I don't care if she stays," Drea says.

I, on the other hand, am not so sure. But she ends up staying anyway.

.   .   .

We sit in a triangle on the floor and clasp hands, focusing on the candle in the center of us. "Close your eyes," I tell them, "but don't lose sight of the flame. Embrace it—its light, its energy. Picture it all around you. Breathe the light's energy in and out, conscious of the action, grateful for it."

We practice the guided breathing for several minutes, until the energy in the room falls like snow all around us. Until we're ready to begin. "Drea," I say, opening my eyes, "I realize it's going to be hard for you to trust me after I lied to you, but you have to believe me." I break our embrace to reach into my night table drawer for the three cards from her reading. I spread them out in front of her.

"You saved them?"

I nod. "Before I tell you what they mean, you have to remember there's a reason we've been given this glimpse into the future. We're destined to change it."

"O-kay," she says, not okay.

"The Ace and the Five of Clubs are for a letter and package you're going to receive. The Ace of Spades is the death card. There's a good chance that this letter, this package, or both could be linked by death. Your death."

"*What*?!" Drea asks. "What are you saying?"

"Just be careful," I say. "Be careful of any gifts or packages you receive."

"What does that mean? I'm going to get a *gift* and there's going to be a *bomb* inside?"

"Drea . . . " I don't want to say it, but it has to be said, and so I just do. "I think someone might be trying to kill you."

"*What*?!" So loud and breathy that it almost extinguishes the candle flame.

"The recurring nightmare I've been having . . . it's a premonition. About you."

"*Me*?"

"I've had them before. Three years ago. About Maura, the little girl I used to baby-sit." I look away. I don't want to continue, don't want to admit what happened, even though it haunts me every day.

Because it haunts me every day.

"In the nightmares, she was trapped in a shed. A crammed, dark shed with cracked cement walls. I could see her, her back toward me, lying on a bench, sort of curled up like she was asleep. But she was scared. I could feel how scared she was, like I was living it in a way. And for weeks I had these horrible, aching headaches."

Drea clutches her pillow. I can tell she believes me. She reaches into her fridge and hands me a fresh can of soda.

"Thank you," I say. It's just what I need. The artificial sweetness stings the inside of my mouth like icy cold Pop Rocks. "As the dreams went on," I continue, "I was tempted to do something, to tell the police, but it just sounded so stupid in my head. So stupid because when you looked outside, there was Maura, playing on her swings, clothes-pinning cards to the spokes of her bike to make that motoring sound. So I just told myself it was a dumb dream, and soon it would pass."

"And what happened?" Drea asks.

I bite my lip to steady the shake, and then I just say it. "Someone took her. She was gone."

"What do you mean, *gone*?" Amber asks.

"I mean *gone*. Missing." I wipe the drizzle from the corner of my eyes.

"Where?"

The words about what happened have been building up inside my head for a couple years now, and I know I have to tell them. I've read the books. I've heard the experts on *Oprah*. If I want to make the horrible thing seem less horrible, less powerful and controlling in my life, I need to face it and tell it to others. As horrible as the memory is, I know it's so much worse just festering inside my head. I take a deep breath in, exhale for three full beats, and then finally say it. "Maura was killed."

"*What? How?*" Amber asks.

I feel the tears drip down the creases of my face. "They found her body in a tool shed just two blocks from our neighborhood. It was this psycho guy who did it. They caught him pretty quickly. People had seen him around. Apparently he used to watch her every morning when her mother walked her to school."

"Yeah, but it wasn't your fault," Amber pipes. "You couldn't have known. I mean, how many people take their dreams that seriously? Plus, you said you saw her in some shed. You didn't see *who* took her. Or *where* the shed was exactly. It probably wouldn't even have helped."

I made up excuses like that when it happened, but excuses don't take away anything, especially blame. I wasn't the one to make those kinds of judgments, to say that my dreams probably wouldn't have helped.

Maybe they would have saved Maura's life.

"Anyway," I breathe, "now I'm having nightmares about Drea."

"So, is Chad still gonna ask me out someplace and then cancel?"

I nod and wipe at my face. "Probably the next time you talk to him."

Amber rests a hand on Drea's back to comfort her. I can tell Drea's scared. I'm scared too. Scared for Drea. Scared that history will repeat itself. I mean, sure, my mother was there to comfort me after Maura's death, was there to wrap her arms around my shoulders and try and make the shaking stop, but she just didn't understand the way Gram would have. She didn't understand the nightmares or guilt.

Or why, being *her* daughter, I was so much like Gram in the first place.

I take a deep breath, unscrew the bottle of lavender oil, and pour two drops into the mixing pot. "To purity and to clarity," I say. "This spell is to help make my dreams more clear, so I can predict the future before it happens." I unclasp the sterling silver chain from around my neck and dip it into the oil. With a finger, I spiral it around the bottom of the pot three times, making sure it gets fully submerged.

"What does that do?" Amber asks.

"The color silver will help give me insight as I travel in the astral."

"Sounds kinky," Amber says.

"The astral is our dreams." I close my eyes and concentrate on it. "Silver chain, as each link binds the next and forms a string around my neck, so may the links of my psychic dreams bind to unify the visions of my subconscious mind." I open my eyes and, with the yellow crayon, write the question WHAT ARE MY NIGHTMARES TRYING TO WARN ME? across Drea's diary page. "Yellow is for clarity of thought," I say, folding the page up into a palm-sized square and slipping it into the pencil case that I use for a dream bag. I glance a moment at Drea, at the dark, grayish aura that cloaks her hair and shoulders.

"What's that?" Amber asks, pointing at the branch of rosemary.

I pick up the sprig, its fresh, pointed needles like a Christmas tree branch. "This will help purify the energy around me so I can remember." I pluck twenty-eight needles from the branch, the number of days in a moon's full cycle, and sprinkle them into the pot. "Rosemary, hold strong my dreams all full of wonder, as I lay me down to slumber."

I concentrate on the mixture and then pull the silver necklace from the pot. "Will you help me?" I hand the necklace to Drea and gesture for her to fasten it. The chain hangs around my neck at the collarbones, the lavender oil drooling down my skin, a few stray rosemary needles at my throat.

"So, are we done?" Amber asks.

"Not quite," I say, diffusing the candle with a snuffer.

"Why don't you blow it out?" Amber asks.

"Because that would confuse the energies and cause a negative backlash."

"Oh, yeah, right," Amber says, rolling her eyes.

I mix the oil and rosemary in the pot with my fingers, and then pour the mixture into the dream bag. I wait a few seconds for the candle to cool a bit, for the pool of liquid wax around the wick to solidify. Then I scoop the clump out and plant it inside the dream bag.

"And you said *I* had weird habits," Amber says.

I zip the bag back up and slide it into my pillowcase. "Repeat after me," I say, clasping their hands. "With the strength of the moon and stars and sun, as I do, it shall be done. Blessed be the way!"

Drea and Amber repeat the chant and we unclench hands. I lay down in bed and touch the silver chain around my neck, the sweet, flowery smell of rosemary lingering on my skin and the nubs of my fingers. "Good night," I say.

I pull the covers up to my chin and concentrate on the dream bag inside my pillow and the question inside, confidant that they will soon help reveal the truth behind my nightmares.

They have to.

Nine

Before I'm able to nod off to sleep, Amber announces she's crashing in our room, claiming that all my nightmare-talk has wigged her out. I'm nervous at first. It's hard enough trying to hide my bedwetting from Drea, never mind Amber, who'll be sleeping on a futon wedged in between our beds. But sleeping isn't even an issue because as soon as her head skims the pillow, Amber starts snoring—chest-heaving, wide-mouthed, nostril-flaring snores.

When the alarm clock vibrates beneath my pillow, alerting me that it's 5 A.M., I sit up, fish a sweatshirt from the growing pile of dirty clothes on the floor, yank it over my head, and head out to the laundry room to retrieve my stuff.

The campus is still asleep as I make my way over there, but the woods are not. I can hear birds chirping away from the tops of trees and the nests of bushes as the morning dew lifts itself from trunks and branches and stretches out into the morning air. It's almost peaceful, almost worth getting up so early on a school day after not having slept all night. *Almost.*

When I get to the washroom, I'm filled with this delicious sense of peace, of being one with nature. But then I swing the door open and everything changes. There's no laundry in sight.

I hurry across the speckled linoleum floor to the machine I used last night. I hold my breath and flip the lid open.

Empty.

I begin flinging open and slamming shut the lids of all the other washers and dryers, hoping that maybe someone merely moved my stuff. But it's nowhere.

Someone must have taken it.

I pick up the campus phone on the wall and call security, thinking that maybe someone turned my laundry in to lost-and-found. No luck. They ask me if I want to make a formal complaint, but considering how that would sound, I politely decline. I'm hoping someone just made an innocent mistake and grabbed my laundry by accident. Hoping that whoever that is doesn't recognize the stuff as mine.

When I get back to the dorm, it's 5:30, and Drea and Amber are still asleep. I crawl back into bed and drag a pillow over my ear. But it isn't enough to block out Amber's snoring, and it isn't enough to muffle the blare of the phone.

"Hello?" I say, dragging the receiver up to my ear.

Silence.

"Hel-lo?" I repeat.

Still nothing, so I hang up.

"Who was it?" Drea asks, rolling over in bed.

"Probably that freakazoid you've been talking to. Who the hell is he, Drea? And why is he so psycho?"

Amber lets out this pain-filled moan. She scooches up in bed, her orange pigtails sticking out like Pippi Longstocking. "What's all the drama?"

The phone rings again. Drea goes to answer it, but Amber intercepts. "Hello? Drea and Stacey's Love Shack."

I have never seen anyone wake up so fast. There's already a wide and cheeky smile stretched across her freckly cheeks. "*Quelle coincidence, monsieur,*" she says into the phone. "We were just talking about you last night." She winks overtly at the two of us. "Funny you should call at this early hour, though. Couldn't sleep? Something keeping you up?"

"Who is it?" I mouth.

"It's Chad." She fans her eyebrows up and down and blows kisses in Drea's direction. "What am I doing here?" she says into the phone. "Couldn't tell you. I've been known to sleepwalk on occasion."

Drea extends her hand for the phone, but Amber avoids it. "Never know where I'll end up," she continues. "Better keep your door locked."

"Give it to me. *Now!*" Drea tries snatching the phone, but Amber's too quick. She jumps up and scurries to the opposite side of the room.

"Huh?" Amber covers her non-receiver ear to block us out. She turns to Drea. "He wants to know if you got his e-mail."

Drea springs from her bed to check.

"He wants to know if you did your psychology homework," Amber says.

Drea nods.

"Well, then, can he, like, borrow it? It's due first period."

Drea's smile wilts, but she nods anyway. She turns away to click on his e-mail.

"Get out!" Amber laughs into the phone. "You guys are *too* funny."

Drea spins around, her white-knuckled fists digging into the groove below her rib cage. "Give me the phone, now!"

"*Breakfast*, huh?" Amber repeats into the phone. "Is that what they're calling it these days? Drea, he wants you to meet him for *breakfast* this morning to study. How's your schedule, babe?" Amber shoots Drea an exaggerated wink.

Drea claps in silence. She plunges into her closet in search of the most perfectly ironed uniform. She pulls one out and holds it up for show. I give her the okay sign with my fingers. Navy blue and green plaid bib-jumpers, white collar-blouses underneath, and navy-blue knee socks. How good *could* they be?

"She's already picking out her clothes," Amber tells Chad. She coils the phone cord around her feet; one sock decorated with cow spots, the other with scattered pictures of various types of cheese. "She just can't wait till senior year when she can wear green knee socks. Just one of the many senior privileges."

Drea whips a Scooby Doo slipper at Amber's head.

"Gotta go, Chaddy Patty. You know how it goes, people to do, things to see. Ciao, ba-by." Amber hangs up, stands, and pinches a three-finger wedge from her pajama crack. "I'm starving. Anyone for food?"

"The card reading was right," I say. "Chad just asked Drea to breakfast."

"He's not gonna cancel," Drea says.

"Yeah," Amber says, "he needs your homework."

"Great." Drea peels the foil down from her chocolate bar and nibbles at her frustration. "Most guys want me for my looks. Chad wants me for my brain."

"Sucks for you," Amber says.

I ignore the rest of their banter and take a seat by the corner window. I end up staring out at the tall maple tree in the distance, the one me and Chad christened at the end of last year, just after finals, when he and Drea were broken up.

We sat beneath it, eating peanut butter and banana sandwiches and talking about our plans for the summer.

"Are you cold?" he asked, referring to the goose flesh on my arm, running a finger over the skin.

I shook my head and noticed that he was staring at my mouth. "You missed some peanut butter," he said.

How elegant. I licked the corner of my mouth and felt a peanut globule hit against my tongue. "Better?"

He nodded.

"I'm such a dainty eater." I looked away to hide the baked-apple heat I knew was visible all over my face.

"You're beautiful."

I looked at him, expecting to hear the butt of the joke. But instead he slipped his hand down my arm and cradled my fingers.

"Drea's beautiful," I said. "I'm—"

"Beautiful," he finished. He turned my chin with his finger, so I would look at him, and smiled like he really meant it. "I've always thought so." He brushed away the few dark strands that had fallen into my eyes, and glanced down again at my lips. "Is this okay?"

I nodded and felt him lean in closer. I closed my eyes, anticipating the kiss, and then felt it warm and fruity against my lips.

On our long walk back to reality that day, I told him I wanted to keep the kiss a secret, that I didn't want to hurt Drea. I wanted the memory to stay forever perfect in my mind, where no one could ruin it.

He told me he had been waiting to kiss me for a whole year.

But now it's me who's waiting.

"Earth to Stacey," Amber shouts, plucking me off the blissful path of memory lane. "If this whole card thing is right, then Chad has less than two hours to cancel Drea's date, right?"

I nod.

"So what happens if you're wrong about the prediction?" Drea asks, her arm loaded down with school uniforms.

"I guess I could be wrong about it all."

But I know I'm not. I turn to glance back out the window. That's when I see him. Again. The man from the night before. "He's back!" I shout.

"Who is?" Drea asks. But then she sees and drops the uniforms to the floor.

He's standing out on the grass, only a few yards away. He looks straight up at us and smiles.

"What a freak!" Amber says.

"Should we do something?" Drea asks.

"Like what?" I say.

"Call security."

"They'll never listen," Amber says. "They think we're nutty."

"Thanks to you," I say.

He takes a step closer and points in our direction. I look at Amber and Drea, but can't tell who he means, who his eyes are focused on, if it's me. I squint to focus harder. But before I can figure it out, he tilts his cap to salute us, and then simply walks away.

Ten

"Are you ready?" Drea is standing by the door of our room, waiting for me, doing a last-minute vanity inspection in the mirror. She drapes her monogrammed towel around her neck and pulls her hair forward over her shoulders. "Remind me to make an appointment later to get my eyebrows waxed." She runs a finger over the invisible fuzz between her eyes. "Let's go. All the showers are going to be taken."

But now that Amber's gone, I want to talk.

"Looks like Chad and I are still on for this morning." She winds a long strand of wavy blond around her fingers, her nails freshly painted in corn yellow.

"Looks like," I say, practically biting through my tongue. Chad still has a whole hour to cancel. And I know he will. I grab the towel from the foot of my bed and drape it around my shoulders. "Drea, before we go, there's something I need to ask you about."

"What?"

"That guy who keeps calling you. Why were you upset the last time he called?"

"Who says I was upset?"

"I know you, Drea. Who is he and why were you upset?"

She sighs. "He's a friend, okay? We just had a misunderstanding."

"About what?"

"He just thought I was seeing someone, but I'm not, so there's no problem."

"What does that mean? Are you two a couple?"

"I don't have time for this. Are you coming or not?" She jiggles her basket full of shampoo products and shower gels.

"Not," I say. "Not until we talk about this."

"Fine," she says. "Then I guess I'll see you later." She closes the door behind her.

I plop down on my bed, a serious headache creeping across my temples. Sometimes I wish my problems could be solved as simply as that scene in the movie *Grease*. The one where the diner morphs into a chunk of heaven. Where Frankie Avalon swoops down from a sparkling, light-filled sky and plays guardian angel for Frenchy, who needs advice about beauty school.

I could use some advice, too.

I roll over and glance toward the broken window. There's a clicking sound coming from just outside it.

"Drea?" I sit up. Maybe she forgot something.

The noise continues.

I move off the bed and grab the baseball bat from behind the door. I sling it over my shoulder, batter-up style, and wait. A whistling now—slow and steady and separated by human breaths. I take a few steps toward the sound, but then it seems to travel over to the corner window, the one that isn't broken. I follow it, noticing the window is open a crack.

"Stacey," says a voice. "I can see you. Can see your pretty plaid pajamas."

I take another step, my heart beating down the door of my chest, forcing me to stop, take a deep breath. I root myself in place, secure my hands around the baseball bat, and mentally prepare myself for his next move.

And there it is—a hand smacks up against the glass, the fingers squirming and kneading their way upward, toward the window frame, to open it wider.

I lean forward to see the figure below. It looks up at me, almost startled, its face covered by a white hockey mask, and suddenly I feel like I've been plopped onto the set of *Friday the 13th* and at any minute now a six-inch knife will come plunging through the window.

The hand curls into a fist and knocks against the glass. And then he starts laughing. A dead giveaway. I'd know that

Kermit-the-frog laugh anywhere—head, bobbing; mouth, arched open; and zero sound coming out.

Chad.

He flips the mask off and breathes aloud, Jason-from-*Friday-the-13th* style. "I can see you, Stacey," he repeats, still laughing.

"I hate you, Chad."

He smooshes his lips against the glass, but he still looks good. Fresh-out-of-bed good—his sandy-blond hair still sticking up in the back, a bedsheet-pattern line against his cheek, tiny points of fresh, golden hair sprouting from his chin. Sexily delicious.

"Where's your sense of humor?"

I start to pull the window shade down to block him out. I don't want to talk to him right now. I look awful. I feel awful. And I despise jokes like this.

"Wait a minute," he says. "I'm sorry, okay?"

It's hard to resist since he looks so scrumptious, standing on tiptoes, a glob of white toothpaste gathered in the corner of his mouth. An imaginary bubble blows out from my head. In it, the two of us have woken up together; he's sneaking out, and this is our secret.

I pop the thought out of my head with a pin of reality and push the window open. "What are you doing here?"

"I was actually looking for Drea."

"She's showering. Why?"

"We were supposed to meet for breakfast. I was gonna help her with her psych homework."

"Really? I thought it was the other way around."

"I help her, she helps me." He winks. "What's the difference?" He hoists his elbows up on the sill to peer into the room. "You girls are slobs. Worse than us bachelors."

I smooth my hands over my hair and try to subtly pinch my cheeks for color. "I'll tell her you came by."

"What's the matter? You want me to go so soon?" Chad dangles his hand off the sill, inside the room, allowing me to catch a glance of the tiny points of boy-hair on his knuckles. "Can I come in?" he asks.

"Why?"

"What do you mean *why*? To hang out for a while. To talk. We don't get to talk as much as we did last year."

It's true that we don't. But it hasn't exactly been the same between us since that day when we kissed. I look at him, from his long, curly lashes to the pout in his mouth, and feel a million tiny bottle-rockets go off in my heart, just remembering that kiss.

"Please," he says. "With peanut butter and banana sandwiches on top?"

I feel my cheeks turn warm, like bowls of chowder. He's thinking about it too. It doesn't surprise me that he's thinking about it. What surprises me is that he's *admitting* that he's thinking about it, and that's something altogether different.

He *wants* me to know that he's thinking about it.

A part of me wants to let him in. Another part wants to close the window and yank the shade down over his face, once and for all. I swallow both parts down in one bittersweet gulp and say, "That's probably not a good idea. Madame Discharge usually makes her rounds sometime around now."

He nods, disappointment brimming in those luscious, greeny-blue eyes.

I bite the side of my cheek and search my brain for something to say. Anything. "So, who told you we like horror?"

"A little bird," he says, sticking his chest out. It takes me a moment to notice that he's wearing his old hockey jersey, the one that was tacked up over the broken window.

"Hey, you have your jersey. When did you get it back? Someone took it from our room."

"Sure they did."

"They did," I say. "We came back late last night and it was missing." I look back at the broken window, at the image of Scooby Doo posing from the beach towel tacked up over the hole—Amber's addition.

Chad pulls the hockey mask back over his face and breathes like Darth Vader. "This was just my way of getting you guys back after your failed attempt at scaring me. Better luck next time."

"What are you talking about? We didn't try to scare you."

He lifts the mask from his face. "You didn't?"

I shake my head.

"Then who put the jersey in my mailbox?" He tugs a sheet of notebook paper from his back pocket. "This was attached to it."

I take the note. There are large block letters written with red marker across the page: STAY AWAY FROM HER. I'M WATCHING YOU.

"Whatever," he says. "Probably just one of the guys, playing a joke. Look, I gotta go before security catches me. Maybe I can come in some other time."

"Maybe," I nod, still clutching the note in my hand.

"Can you just tell Drea I can't make it for breakfast after all? Hockey practice."

I swallow down the ball of impending doom I feel lodged in my throat, and manage a slight nod.

"Tell her Donovan's gonna be in the room, so she can just e-mail him the assignment, and I'll have him print it out and give it to me before class."

My head fuzzes over with questions, but instead of asking any I just say "Okay."

"Thanks, Stacey. Tell Dray thanks, too. I owe her big time. Oh, and can you tell her to make sure she changes her answers around a bit? Wouldn't want the teacher to think we're cheating." He winks.

I wave goodbye before shutting the window and locking it.

There, it happened. He canceled. The cards predicted correctly.

Eleven

I whip the door of the shower room open and boog it across the red clay floor in search of Drea. There are a few girls waiting in line for a shower stall, their arms full of fruity shampoo and bars of soap, but no Drea. I visually scour the pairs of feet sticking out from beneath each curtain, in search of Drea's pink jelly shoes. I notice a pair of Oscar the Grouch flip-flops, standing in the last stall. "Amber? Is that you?" I jiggle the curtain.

"Get lost," says a throaty voice that definitely isn't Amber's.

I round the corner by the sinks and there's Drea, in front of the mirror, scrunch-drying her hair with a blow dryer.

She clicks the dryer off. "What's wrong?"

"Are you okay?" I'm all out of breath. I look over her shoulder at Veronica Leeman, who pretends to brush her teeth a few sinks away even though it's so completely obvious that she's eavesdropping.

"Are *you* okay?" Drea asks.

"Get your stuff and let's go," I say. "We need to talk."

"What-ev-er." Drea focuses back in the mirror and plucks a salmon-pink lipstick from her makeup pouch. She smears it on and blows obnoxious air kisses toward Veronica. "Chad just *loves* this color on me."

Everyone knows Veronica would give up using hair spray for a whole year just to have one date with Chad. Drea smiles at me, proud of her own bitchiness.

"Actually, Chad can't make it for breakfast," I say, savoring every syllable. *I* can be a bitch too.

Veronica spits a mouthful of toothpaste out in Drea's sink, a speck of peppermint spooge landing against Drea's cheek.

"Watch it!" Drea squeals, swiping the dribbles with a cotton ball.

Veronica gets right up into Drea's face. "If I catch you and your loser friends flashing my dad again, you'll have *me* to answer to."

"What are you talking about?" Drea asks.

"That was my father last night outside your room," Veronica continues. "He was looking for my room, and unfortunately found yours. Your room *is* the one on the ground floor, all the way to the right, facing the lawn, isn't it? Are you girls that hard up that you have to resort to middle-aged men?"

"Is your father that hard up that he has to resort to peeping in the windows of teenage girls?"

"Screw you," Veronica says. "For your information, he works the late shift and had to swing by my room to pick up some keys. There wasn't anyone working the front desk."

Drea squirts a few puffs of perfume in Veronica's direction to ward her off. "Well, he must have liked what he saw, because he came back for more this morning."

"To drop the keys back off—not that it's any of your business." Veronica walks away and Drea and I look at each other and burst out laughing.

"It figures she would have a wacko-perv for a father," Drea says.

"I can't believe that was him," I say.

"Wait," Drea rebounds. "What do you mean Chad can't make it?"

"He said something about having an early hockey practice," I say. "He wants you to e-mail the assignment to Donovan so he can print it out and give it to Chad before class."

"Why isn't Donovan going to the hockey practice? He's the star center." Drea hurls her lipstick into the sink. "I'm so sick of him lying to me and blowing me off. This is just like last week. He gave me some pathetic story about visiting his sick grandmother."

"He *did* have his hockey mask with him," I say. "You know what this means though, don't you? The cards were right. He canceled."

"I have more important things to think about than cards."

"More important than your life?"

Drea tries to push her way past me, but I grab her arm and spin her around. "Your spoiled brat routine isn't going to work this time," I say. "I'm going to help you whether you like it or not."

She stares at me a few seconds, as though not wanting to listen but too scared to run away. "I can't deal with this right now."

"Well, I'm sorry, but you don't have a choice. You're my best friend and I don't want anything to happen to you."

I lead Drea into a bathroom stall for privacy, pull the now-mangled note from the center of my palm, and drop it into hers.

"What's this?"

"Just open it," I say. "It was attached to Chad's hockey jersey. He got it back. It was stuffed into his mailbox with the note."

"'Stay away from her. I'm watching you'?" Drea reads. "Wait, I'm confused; I thought *I* was supposed to get the note."

"You will," I say. "Another one. Addressed to you. I'm sure of it."

"Who's the 'her' in the note?" she asks.

"Who do you think?"

Drea smiles. "It's me, isn't it."

"It's not a compliment, Drea. This is serious. Whoever sent this note to Chad is trying pretty hard to make sure he stops hanging around you. Chad might even be in danger himself."

Drea's smile wilts. "That doesn't make sense. Why would anyone want to hurt Chad?"

"Because whoever this is wants you all to himself."

"So, you're sure it's a guy?"

"Who knows? You've pissed off enough girls around here." I spread the paper out on the wall and smooth my fingers over it to feel the grains. There's a slight vibration coming from the word "her." I trace the letters with my finger and concentrate on each one. Then I close my eyes and bring the paper up to my nose.

"What?" Drea asks. "What is it?"

"Lilies," I say. "Like in my dream. There were lilies."

"What do lilies have to do with anything?" she asks. "They're just flowers."

"Lilies are the death flower."

"You're scaring me."

"We're in this together," I say, taking her hand and holding it. "If we can predict the future, we can change it."

"So much for fate."

"We make our own fate," I say. "I'm not going to let anything happen to you."

"Promise?"

I nod and think of Maura.

"You're my best friend," she says.

I lean over and give her what we both need, the biggest hug.

"Can I just make one small request?" Drea asks.

"Anything."

"Can we get out of this bathroom stall now?"

"Totally," I giggle. "We still have a half hour before classes—skipping breakfast, that is."

"I don't think I can eat."

"Let's go back to the room and make a plan."

By the time we emerge from the stall, the entire bathroom has emptied out. All except for what awaits us.

It sits across the width of the sink. A large, rectangular box, wrapped in cherry-red paper, with a silver bow. There's a card attached on top with Drea's name written in the same red block lettering as Chad's note.

I reach for Drea's hand, but it's trembling over her mouth. A wheezing sound sputters from her throat, like she's having trouble finding her breath. "Drea, are you okay?"

But her eyes aren't even focused on the package. They're focused on the salmon-pink words that are sprawled across the mirror. Someone wrote them using the lipstick she placed to her lips only minutes ago: I'M WATCHING YOU, DREA.

twelve

"Drea?" I cup her shoulder. "Are you okay?"

She manages a nod but continues to wheeze. I take her hand and lead her away from the mirror, away from the pink smear of lipstick scribbled across.

This seems to help her a bit. After a few seconds, her gasping becomes less violent, less desperate. "We'll get through this," I assure her, but I'm not even sure she hears me. Her eyes are closed, like she's concentrating hard on catching her breath. "I'm here."

But so was the person who left this gift. I look toward the door. I absolutely hate it that the shower room is on the ground floor of our building. If the exit door out in the hallway is unlocked, which it often is when the maintenance people are cleaning, it's like anybody can just walk in here from outside.

I wonder if anyone saw who did this. If it has anything to do with that guy Drea's been talking to. But maybe it's not even a *him*. Maybe it's some girl who has a crush on Chad, but can't get to him because of Drea.

Maybe someone like me.

I brainstorm a mental list of all the girls who've crushed on Chad during the past year. But, aside from myself and Drea, the only one I can think of is Veronica Leeman. Veronica, who was here only minutes ago, who spat out her toothpaste at Drea and bitched at us for flashing her father.

"Drea, are you all right?" I squeeze her china-doll fingers.

She nods. "Panic attack. I haven't had one since middle school."

"Do you want to go see the nurse?"

"No. I just want to know who did this. Let's open it," she says, referring to the package.

"Are you sure?"

She nods and wipes the trickle of tears that's sliding down her cheeks. "I have to know." She slowly meanders her way to the wrapped-up gift, then turns to look at me. "Will you help me?"

"Do you want me to open it?"

She nods. "I'll open the card, you open the present. Deal?"

"Deal." I sit down on the bench with the package on my lap—the small, white envelope with Drea's name, facing up. I deposit the envelope into her hand and watch as she tears it open with her thumb. She pulls out a folded piece of lined paper, the jagged edges freshly torn from someone's spiral notebook.

She unfolds it, smoothes out the creases, and reads the message. "This doesn't make sense." She's shaking her head and scrunching up her face.

"What does it say? Can I see it?"

But she doesn't move or answer.

"Drea?" I pry the note from her fingers. It's written like Chad's—in block lettering with a red marker—FOUR MORE DAYS.

I look at her—at the fresh tears that stain her cheeks. I wrap my arms around her shoulders and rub the length of her hair and back, the way my grandmother used to hug me. "We don't have to open the box now," I whisper. "We can wait until after school, when we feel better. Or I can open it by myself later."

"No," she says, wiping at her face. "Open it now. I have to know now."

I nod, fully understanding how she feels. I have to know too.

I pull the ribbon free of the package, then slowly work at the wrapping, untaping the panels with care, trying to sense any vibrations coming from the paper. When the package is finally free, lying across my lap is a long, white cardboard box. I smile, somewhat relieved, but I have no idea why. I look up at Drea—she shares that same look. I remove the cover and look down at the contents: four freshly cut lilies.

"Lilies," Drea says, swallowing. "The death flower. Isn't that what you said?"

I nod. There's no use lying anymore. Strength comes with honesty.

"So, four lilies. Four days till death, right?" Drea's lips tremble, but instead of crying she starts laughing, hysterical laughter. She plucks a lily from the box and bats it against her nose. "I guess he was too cheap to spring for a dozen. Or maybe a dozen would have been too long for him to wait. Hey, if he does it by Friday, I won't have to take my trig test. You think I could ask him to move it up?"

I touch Drea's hand and rub her back, watch these simple gestures convert laughter into tears. She cups her hands over her face and collapses into my arms. I don't know what to do. I don't know what to say to make it better. I can only try to stop the danger before it happens. I rock her back and forth on the bench and feel a nerve at the back of my neck tense up.

The sound of footsteps is coming toward us from the long row of showers. I stand, accidentally stepping on the wrapping paper and causing a slight rustle.

The footsteps stop.

Drea grasps at my arm to hold me back. I place my finger up to my lips to shush her, take a step closer to the sinks, and ready myself to peer around the wall.

Maybe the person who left the gift is still here, waiting.

"Stacey," Drea whispers. "What are you doing?"

I peer around the corner but I don't see anyone, just a row of empty shower stalls, the curtains drawn open. I peel Drea's grasp from around my forearm and begin down the row of stalls. That's when I notice—the two at the end have their curtains drawn closed.

There's a clanking sound, like metal, coming from the last stall. I reach inside my pocket for my key ring and prepare the sharpest key to protect myself. "I know you're there," I call out. "Come out and show yourself."

A pair of feet—black leather clunk-shoes—takes a step closer to the curtain.

"Come out!" I demand.

"Stacey!" Drea shouts.

A white chiffon scarf pokes out from behind the curtain and waves back and forth. I look closer. The scarf has yellow ducks patterned across the edges. It can only be one person.

"I surrender," Amber yells, jumping out from the stall. "Just don't hurt me."

I let out a long, relief-filled breath and release the key from my grip. "Amber, what are you doing here?"

Drea emerges from behind the wall to join us. "You scared us half to death."

"Sorry," she says, banging her metal Daffy Duck lunch box against the wall. "Just having a little peek-a-boo fun. Didn't think you'd take it so seriously."

"How else are we supposed to take it?" I ask.

She ties the duck scarf around her neck so that it sticks out slightly from the collars of her uniform, just enough to piss off Mr. Gunther, her first period algebra teacher, and score her a big, fat detention.

"I was looking for you guys," she says. "Coming to breakfast?"

"How long have you been here?" Drea asks.

"I don't know. Like, two minutes."

"Did you see anyone coming this way, carrying a gift?" Drea asks.

"You got it?"

Drea nods.

"Holy shit." Amber's eyes slam shut for emphasis, exposing two more ducks, penciled onto her lids with brown and yellow eyeliner. "What was it?"

"We'll explain later," I say. "I don't want to talk here."

"This is so cool," Amber says. "It's like some bad horror movie or something. I feel like—who's that chick from the original *Halloween*?"

"You mean Jamie Lee Curtis?" I say.

"Yeah, I feel like her."

"Amber," I say, "this is serious. It's not for your entertainment."

She looks at Drea, close to tears. "Oh yeah. Sorry, Dray. I can be such an insensitive beetle sometimes."

"Cockroach," Drea corrects.

"Right." Amber's cell phone rings from inside her lunch box. She ignores it out of courtesy. "Just tell me whatever I can do to help, and I will."

"We need to make a pact," I say. "Right here and now." I extend my hand in the air, facedown. Drea places hers over mine. Amber does the same, until our hands make a six-inch-high pig pile. "Close your eyes and repeat after me," I say, feeling the warmth of their hands enveloping my own. "To secrecy."

"To secrecy," Drea says.

"To secrecy," Amber repeats.

"And to honesty and strength," I say.

"And to honesty and strength," they both repeat in turn.

"Or death will surely part us," I say.

"Or death will surely part us," Drea says.

"Or death will surely part us," Amber hiccups.

We open our eyes and lock them on each other for several seconds without saying a word. Then we take our hands back.

thirteen

Breakfast is already over by the time we make it out of the shower room. So, we wait—the longest school day of the year—until after classes to go back to the dorm and make a plan. PJ asked to come over, but we told him we needed some female-bonding time. He didn't argue. He only promised to come by and eavesdrop.

We sit in a circle on the floor, a chunky purple candle in the middle. I'm beyond tired at this point, can barely focus.

I need time to make a plan, but I also need time to sleep, to live out my nightmares and figure out what everything means.

Amber busies her fingers by plucking the lily petals from their stems and dropping them into the orange clay pot.

"Leave the stems to the side," I tell her. "We may need them later."

Drea grabs a fresh chocolate bar from her fridge. She peels the wrapper down and takes a bite, and for just one evil moment, I wonder why all that sugar never makes its way to the backs of her thighs.

"Do you think we should tell campus security about the note?" Amber asks.

"No," Drea says. "They'll call my parents and then I'll have security officers following me to the bathroom. No, thanks."

"Maybe we should," I say.

"Yeah, we'll just tell them that somebody gave me flowers along with a card that says 'four days' on it. *So* threatening," she mocks. "Four days could mean anything. It could be four more days until I get my period, for god's sake. Four days until hell freezes over."

"Is that what you really think?" I ask.

"I don't know, Stace. What do you think? Maybe you should call the police. Maybe you should tell them all about your premonitions and the symbolism of lilies. They won't think we're crazy or anything."

"Why are you being like this?" I ask.

"Maybe it has something to do with the fact that someone wants to kill me."

I grab the backpack from my bed and pull three lemons (courtesy of the cafeteria lady) out from the side pocket. "No. I mean, why are you so against going to the police?"

Amber pauses from petal-plucking to hear the answer as well.

"Because maybe I know who it is."

"You do?"

"Maybe."

"Who?" I ask.

"Maybe it's Chad."

"*Chad*? Why would *Chad* do this?"

"Why else? To scare me, so I'll go running to him. To get me back, basically."

"That's so dumb," Amber says.

"What can I say? He's a boy. Maybe this is his little way of bringing us closer."

"You don't, like, *really* believe that, do you?" Amber stops her eyes mid-roll, speaking toward the crack in the ceiling.

"What else am I supposed to think?" Drea huddles her legs in close and crosses them at the ankle, so they make a valentine heart below her chin.

"If he wanted to get so close to you, then why would he break your breakfast date?" I take the lemons and cut them in half with a plastic knife.

Drea shrugs. She takes a huge bite of chocolate, making it difficult to answer any more questions. I don't think she really believes that Chad is behind this whole thing, but I think that's the only explanation her mind will let her digest right now.

"So, what are we doing with these lilies anyway?" Amber asks, shoving a flower behind her ear.

"Well," I say, grabbing it back, "first we're going to soak them in lemon juice and vinegar. And then we're going to put them into a bottle with pins and needles."

"That's what I thought," Amber says, rolling her eyes. She snatches Drea's chocolate bar mid-bite and breaks off a piece for herself. "I'm starving. Did you see that gelatin slop they were dishing out in the cafeteria today? Total yuck."

"I wasn't hungry," Drea says, grabbing her candy bar back.

I pick up one of the lilies and admire the strong, broad petals, the way they fall open in a perfect bell shape. I trace the silky threads with my fingertips. "The person who left this," I say, "is very close." I close my eyes and slide my thumb and index finger down the length of the stem to feel the smoothness. I can tell it was soaked in water for some time, at least a couple days, and that the end was cut with a delicate hand. I move my fingers upward to feel a leaf. I stop, press it between my fingers and feel at the veins to be sure. The veins travel straight up to the tip, but then taper off into tiny Vs that run east and west. "I feel a shelter of some sort."

"What kind of a shelter?" Drea asks.

I shake my head, frustrated that I can't tell more. I lift the petal to my nose. "Dirt," I nod. "It smells like dirt."

"Well, they did come from a florist," Amber says. "They do, like, have dirt there."

"No," I say, sniffing again. "Dirt. It's all around me." I drop the lily to my lap and sniff my fingers. The earthy scent is everywhere—on my hands, in my clothes, tangled up in my hair.

I close my eyes and try to concentrate on the scent. I picture the powdery brown mass being turned, and over-turned, and then turned again, the color alternating at points—from golden and hazel to dark chestnut, almost black. I press my fingers up to my nostrils and inhale the pinky skin, breathing in every grain of the earthy spirit. I can picture the dirt forming a tall pile of some sort. Cone shaped, like a tepee. "Someone's digging something."

"Like what?" Amber asks.

I open my eyes and shake my head. "I don't know."

"Well, leave it to me to attract some psycho dirt-eater," Drea says.

"Dirt-*digger*," Amber corrects.

I'm almost surprised they're making jokes about it, especially Drea. But it's like that's the only way she can swallow the news and keep it down.

"When did you learn to do that?" Amber asks.

"What?"

"Read things like that?"

"It's weird," I say. "But I think I've always had it, like it was always there, even when I wasn't old enough to accept or understand it. I would touch something and get these mental pictures from it, these intense feelings. It didn't happen all the time; it still doesn't. I used to practice around the house—my mom's keys, a neighbor's watch—and feel nothing. Then I'd be out somewhere, like at a friend's house, and pick up a dishtowel and sense divorce."

"I wouldn't want to know things like that," Drea says.

"I used to feel that way. But I'm trying to think of it as a gift—you know, a way to help people."

"My parents are going to get a divorce," Drea says. "You don't have to go towel-touching to tell me."

"Hey, Stace, can you use that psychic stuff to tell me if Brantley Witherall is going to ask me to prom this year?" Amber grabs her lunchbox-purse and opens it. She takes out her florescent-green cell phone, decorated with tiny ladybug stickers, and the matching phone charger.

"Brantley Witherall, Mr. 'I-love-to-flip-my-eyelids-inside-out-for-my-own-amusement'?" Drea says. "A girl can only dream."

"Maybe I'll just ask Donovan to prom instead. He did smile at me in the cafeteria yesterday." Amber gives a little self-satisfied smirk as she plugs in the phone charger. Even though Drea has absolutely zero interest in Donovan, she still thinks she owns his affection.

"Why do you even need a cell phone?" Drea asks. "You're with us all day long. Who calls you on it?"

"PJ."

"You two should just go back out," Drea says. "He so wants to."

"Wouldn't you just love that?" Amber says.

"What's that supposed to mean?"

"Maybe you're looking to eliminate the competition."

"Please," Drea says. "I hardly think we're playing in the same division."

"Can you guys just stop?" I pull the remaining petals from their stems and mix my fingers through their whiteness. "We're supposed to be working together."

The phone rings, poking a hole in our conversation.

"I'll get it." Amber reaches for the receiver. "Hello? Hellooo?" She waits a couple seconds before clicking the phone off.

"Another prank?" I ask.

Amber shrugs. "Probably PJ. He won't take no for an answer."

"It wasn't PJ," I say. "Was it, Drea?"

"What are you talking about?" Drea asks.

"How many prank calls and threats do we have to get before you start taking this seriously? Are you gonna spill it about this guy or what?"

The phone rings again.

"I'll get it," Drea says.

"Put it on speakerphone," I say. "That way we can all listen."

"No," Drea says. "This has nothing to do with him."

"Well, if it doesn't, then let us listen. If it sounds okay, just switch the speakerphone off and I'll never mention his name again."

"Not that you know his name," Amber corrects.

Drea shrugs. I can tell she sort of wants to do it. I know there's something up with this guy. And I know that's why she wants to keep him a secret.

"Fine," she says. "But get ready to be wrong." She presses the speakerphone button, followed by the receiver button. "Hello?"

"Hi," he says. "It's me." His voice is coarse, like beach sand.

"How are you?" Drea asks.

Silence.

"Hello?" Drea says.

"Don't ever think you're smarter than I am," he says.

"What are you talking about?"

"I know I'm on speakerphone right now. And I know your friends are listening."

"No," Drea says, leaning in closer to the speaker. "It's just me."

"Don't lie to me," he says, his voice stern and cutting.

"What do you want?" I ask, looking toward the window, wondering if he's somewhere, watching.

"This is between Drea and me, Stacey. It has nothing to do with you. Besides, I don't believe in witches."

A ten-pound pause drops in the center of us. Our eyes lock. I know we all must be wondering the same thing: How does he know my name?

"Why are you doing this?" Drea's voice crackles. "I thought we were friends."

"And I thought we were much more than friends. At least that's what you said the other night. But since then, you haven't exactly been faithful."

Drea's cheeks pinken, like roses beneath her skin.

"Did you get my gift?" he asks.

"Those lilies were from you?"

"Four of them," he says. "For the number of days until we meet."

"Why are you being like this? You weren't like this before."

"And neither were you. Four days, Drea. I can hardly wait." *Click.*

"His voice is so familiar," I say.

"Dial star-six-nine," Amber says.

I press the receiver button down and dial, expecting to hear the operator say that the number is blocked. But instead the mechanical voice chants out the numbers. Amber jots them down on the back of her hand with an eyeliner pencil.

"So now what?" Drea asks. "Call him back?"

"Why not?" Amber grabs the phone receiver. "Let this freak know who he's dealing with."

"No, don't." Drea snatches the phone away and holds it under her leg.

"Why?" Amber asks.

"Just wait," she breathes. "I want to wait." She tucks the phone farther under her thigh.

"Wait for what? If we call back right away he might still be there." Amber dabs a bit of the blue eyeliner from her hand and smudges it onto her eyelid like shadow. "Hey, at least we know it's not Chad now. This isn't his number."

The droning of the dial tone off the hook, muffled only slightly by Drea's leg, plays like a continuous scream between the three of us.

"What do you think he meant by saying you haven't been faithful?" I ask. "Do you think he's talking about your breakfast date with Chad?"

"I don't know anything anymore," Drea says.

"Maybe it *is* Chad," Amber says. "Maybe he's jealous at the way you walked off with Donovan in the cafeteria. Maybe he's just using someone else's phone."

"Four days," Drea whispers. She dips her fingers into the pot of petals. "How is all this supposed to help me?"

I take the glass bottle from the window and place it in front of her. It's slender, a bit smaller in size than one of those old-fashioned Coke ones, and was once used to hold sea salt. "It's already been bathed in the moonlight," I tell her.

Drea picks it up and fists the base, hard, as though trying to break it in her hands.

"Drea—" Amber reaches out to touch Drea's forearm. "It's gonna be all right."

I squeeze the lemon sections over the pot of petals, the juice drizzling down in pulp-filled drips. I chase the mixture with three splashes of vinegar from the cap and mix it all up with my fingers, the contents of the pot warming in my hand as the petals become saturated.

Together, Drea and I finger the damp and gooey petals into the spout of the bottle, trying to make sure that all the drips make their way inside.

"Here," I say, handing her a small, wooden container that fits in her palm.

She opens it and looks down at the array of shiny pins and needles.

"Put in as many as you think you'll need to protect yourself," I say.

"Are you serious? I'm supposed to stop this guy with some sewing needles?"

"Just fill it," I say. "It's a protection bottle. Keep it close to you always."

Amber and I watch as Drea feeds all the pins and needles into the bottle. When she's done, I tilt the candle over the spout so the wax drips down to make a seal. "Concentrate on the idea of protection. What does protection mean to you?"

"Probably not the same as what it means to me." Amber fans her eyebrows and flashes us a tiny, neon-green package from her Daffy Duck lunch box.

"That's a temporary tattoo," Drea says. "I was there when you won it out of the machine."

Amber looks at it. "So what? It's the thought that counts."

"Shh," I say. "Drea, you need to concentrate. What thoughts or images come to mind when you think of protection?"

I look at Amber, busy unwrapping the tattoo package. Inside is a picture of a smiling chicken. She rolls her sleeve up and presses it against her forearm.

"Amber—," I say.

"Fine." She tosses the tattoo back into her lunch box.

"Let's hold hands," I say.

I place the protection bottle into the center and we join hands around it, our bodies forming a human triangle. "Close your eyes," I say, "and concentrate on the bottle. I'll start. When I think of protection, I think of the moon. I think of nature: rain, sky, and earth. I think of truth."

"My thoughts exactly." Amber peeps her eye open at the same time I do. "When I think of protection," she begins, "I think of armed guards, multiple armed guards, with strong hands, and big, throbbing, masculine—"

"Amber!" I shout.

"Biceps," she finishes. "What else?"

"When I think of protection," Drea says, "I think of my parents, the way they used to be, when I'd sit between them in their bed, watching movies. When we'd go for walks and each would take my hand. When they loved each other. . . . It just always made me feel safe."

I squeeze Drea's hand, sending the gesture around the circle until it comes back to me through Amber's hand. "Bottle of protection," I say. "Help protect Drea through the powers of Mother Earth, guardian angels, and parental love. Blessed be the way."

"Blessed be the way," Drea says.

"Blessed be the way." Amber opens her eyes and hands the bottle to Drea.

"I'm ready now," Drea says. "Let's call."

"I have a better idea," Amber says. She rummages through her lunch box and extracts an address book. "Stace, do you have a student directory? We can find the number and see who it belongs to. If it's someone on campus, it'll be in there."

"There's one in my night table," Drea says. "But there's, like, twenty pages in the directory. That could take forever."

"Well, I have nothing better to do," Amber says.

I pull the campus directory from the drawer and sit beside Drea with the pages sprawled across our laps. We scan down the long rows of numbers while Amber pages through her address book. "How stupid would this guy have to be to call from his own dorm room?" I say, flipping a page.

"Wait a sec," Amber says. "I have it." She taps her finger over the number.

"Already?" I ask.

"Yeah. It's the pay phone. The one over by the library."

"Can I ask *why* you have pay phone numbers listed in your address book?" Drea asks.

"I just do. You know, in case I ever need it. In case I want someone to call me there. It gets expensive feeding all those quarters in."

"Even though you have a cell phone," Drea says.

"What are you implying?" Amber closes the address book up and tucks it away.

"Seems pretty weird," Drea says. "Some guy wants to kill me and you just happen to carry his number around in your purse."

"It's not *his* number."

"Stop," I say. "This isn't getting us anywhere. We need to trust one another. Remember our pact." I watch as Drea's jaw locks into place.

"I say we go," Amber says. "If this jerk used that phone, he might still be around there. At least *in* the library."

"It could be anybody," Drea says, looking at Amber. "Even two people working together."

"Look," I say. "If we all just go over together . . ."

"Fine." Drea clutches the protection bottle. "Let's go."

fourteen

Drea, Amber, and I run as far as the O'Brian Building, separated from the school library by a single clay tennis court. I'm not sure how effective this is going to be. Only a complete nimrod would be hanging around the same phone he used to make a threatening call. But I suppose there are plenty of nimrods in this world. I look at Amber, case in point. She's hoisted her skirt up, the wool fabric held between her teeth, and is jumping around, yanking her tights into place.

"Okay," Amber says, grabbing at my arm. "We need to act casual. You know, like, we're really here to take out a book or something."

"You? Amber 'I-buy-my-term-papers-off-the-Internet' Foley? Looking for a book?" Drea says. "Whoever it is will know we're onto him as soon as we walk up the stairs."

"For your information, I go to the library at least once a quarter." Amber slides a Hello Kitty pencil behind her ear. "Am I the picture of studiousness or what?"

"You're the picture of something," Drea says. She moves toward the edge of the building and inches her head out to look. "Oh my god. It's Donovan."

"At the library?" I ask.

"No. He's coming out of O'Brian." Drea pulls her head back and draws in a deep breath. "I think he's coming this way."

"So what?" I say. "There's no law against hanging out. We'll just act normal."

Drea scrunches the protection bottle into the waist of her skirt and pulls her sweater over the bulge.

"Good choice," Amber says. "Nobody will ever go looking in there."

Normally, Drea would volley a remark back, but instead she backs herself up against the building and starts breathing all weird, puffing in and out.

"Drea, are you okay?" I ask.

She shakes her head and presses her lips together.

"What's wrong? Do you think it's Donovan?"

"That's the problem." She blots her eyes with her sleeve. "I don't know who it is. I don't know who I can trust anymore." She looks at Amber with giant fish eyes, I think, waiting for a dose of words that will cure any doubt she has. Waiting for Amber to explain all over again why she has the pay phone number in her purse.

But Amber is too busy ignoring Drea to notice.

Donovan rounds the corner and jumps at the sight of us, practically wallpapered to the brick. "Jeez," he says. "You guys scared the crap out of me."

"Hey there, Donovan," Amber says, a smile twisting up on her face.

He nods to her. "What are you guys up to?"

"Do you see any guys here?" Amber gives one last good yank to the back of her tights. "We're *women*."

"Just hanging out," I say, though I'm not even sure why I bother. If Donovan's eyes made brush strokes, Drea would look like a Picasso by now.

"Hey, Drea," he says, kneading the toe of his Doc Marten into the dirt. "Are you coming to the hockey game this weekend? I mean with Chad playing and all."

"I'm not sure. I haven't talked to him yet." Drea folds her hands over the bulge of her sweater and lets out a big breath of air. "Actually we were just running over to the library. We should really get going."

"Sure," he says. "I was just asking because some of us are gonna hang out afterwards. Maybe get something to eat."

"Hockey players *and* food." Amber takes a giant step toward Donovan, landing smack-dab under his nose. "You don't have to ask me twice. What time shall I be there?"

"I don't know," Drea says. "I might have something to do."

"Another time maybe." His eyes hang on Drea a few more seconds before he moves away, not even bothering to say goodbye to Amber or me.

"Oh my god," Amber says, when he's out of earshot. "He *so* wants you." She peers around the corner of the building to watch him walk away. "You don't think it's him, do you?"

"I've known him since the third grade." Drea plucks the protection bottle from under her sweater and secures it in both hands.

Amber tilts her head to size up Donovan's assets from behind. "Not bad. I'd say about an eight on a one-to-ten scale. What do you think, Stace?"

"I think I can't believe he still continues to ask Drea out after all these years."

"Painful," Amber says.

"Did you see the way he studied me?" Drea asks.

"He *always* studies you," I say.

"No. It was different today. More intense."

"He *is* an artist," Amber says. "I just love artists."

"You just love everyone," Drea says.

"Do I sense a note of jealousy?" Amber juts her bosom forward. "The boy *is* fair game. Maybe I'll let him sculpt me."

"I don't think he's into abstracts." Drea kisses the protection bottle and shoves it back into her skirt. "Come on, let's go to the library before I change my mind."

We creep around the side of the building, and even though everything feels as if it's been changed in some way—who we can trust, what we can say, where we can say it—the library appears just as it has on any other day, like a giant brick harmonica dropped down from outer space. The constancy of it comforts me.

We round the corner by the tennis court and there it is. In full view. The pay phone. But it isn't the actual phone we stand there gawking at; it's the person using it.

Chad.

"Oh my god," Drea says. "He's calling home, right? Tell me he's calling his home."

"Right," I say. "Home."

"Right," Amber repeats. "Even though he has a perfectly good phone in his dorm room with an economical calling plan."

"Seriously," I say, "what are the odds that whoever called us would still be on the phone? It could be anybody." I glance around at the swarm of navy-blue-and-green-plaided bodies sitting, stretching, and standing in the quad area.

"Yeah, and maybe if we didn't stop to flirt with Donovan," Drea evil-eyes Amber, "we could have gotten here a lot faster."

"Hey," Amber says, "don't complain. I was just trying to do you a favor."

"Well, don't try so hard next time, okay?"

We continue toward the phone, toward Chad, our eyes burning blisters into his back. He doesn't look like he's talking to anyone, just listening, or waiting for somebody to pick up.

"Chad," Drea says, when we're close enough. "What do you think you're doing?"

He turns and clunks the receiver back down on its cradle. "Oh, hi, guys. What's up?"

"Who were you talking to?" Drea asks.

"Nobody."

"Well, I guess you just hung up on nobody then."

"What *are* you, my mother?" He flips his notebook shut and stacks it atop the heap of books on the shelf.

"I guess I just don't think it's polite to hang up on someone. That's all."

"Well, not that it's any of your business, but I wasn't talking to anyone. They weren't home."

"Who's 'they'?" Amber asks.

Chad ignores her and looks at me, and I feel my cheeks turn into fireballs. "What's up, Stace?"

"Not much," I say, watching his eyes linger at my hips, move past my wobbly knees, and land on my clunky black shoes. Why did I wear socks instead of tights today? I wonder if he notices that the left sock is yanked up at least six inches higher than the right. I cross my legs at the ankle, hoping it offsets how stylistically challenged I am, and glance at Drea. She shoots me a quick dose of the evil eye and then looks away.

"Well," Amber says. "Maybe we should get going." She yawns in Chad's direction. "We were just heading off to the library to study."

"Study?" Chad arches his eyebrows.

"Yeah," Amber says. "You know, that thing you do with books."

"Really?" He folds his arms at us. "How come I don't believe you? What are you guys really up to?"

"*Women*, asshole," Amber says. "Not guys. Not girls. *Women*."

"Don't think for a minute that I don't know what you *women* are doing here."

"What are you talking about?" I say.

A smile curls up his perfectly kissable cheek. "You came for the Olympics of the Mind meeting, right?" He points to a bright orange flyer taped to the wall, calling all first-time brain athletes into the library basement for a meeting.

"Oh, yeah, right," Amber says. "My brain gets enough of a workout in school. The last thing I want to do is use it *after* school."

"That explains a lot," Drea says.

I glance at the iron clock in the middle of the quad. It's just after four o'clock, only twenty minutes after the phone call in our room. "When did you get here?"

"About five minutes ago."

"Did you see anyone using the phone before you?"

"No, why? What's up?"

"Nothing," I say. "I was just supposed to meet someone here. That's all."

"Really?" Chad's eyes narrow on me. "Anyone I should know about?"

"Yeah," Drea bursts out, before I can speak. "Our little Stacey here was just *waiting for someone*. Get the picture?"

"Now get out of the picture," Amber says, fake-smoking her Hello Kitty pencil.

If tearing someone's acrylic nails off, glue and all, and cramming them down her throat didn't look so unattractive, I would probably do just that to Drea right now. She knows exactly what she's doing—burning away any bridge of possibility that exists between me and Chad.

"Three's company," Drea says, twirling a lock of hair around her finger. "So we need to split too, right Amb?"

Amber nods.

"I can take a hint." Chad collects his books and leaves, without even one last minuscule peek in my direction.

Drea elbows me in the ribs when he's gone. "That totally worked. He so believed you were waiting for someone."

"Great," I say.

"So now what?" Amber says. "You don't seriously think it's Chad, do you?"

"He knows something," Drea whispers.

"You don't know that." I watch him as he walks away, until his figure has blended into the sea of matching blue blazers. The last thing I want to believe is that he has anything to do with this.

"What are you staring at?" Drea asks. "Picture will last longer."

"I thought I saw PJ," I say.

"Yeah, right," Drea says. "I don't know why you bother; Chad can be such a jerk. I'm so glad I refused to give him my homework."

"Refused or forgot?" Amber asks. "You were kind of preoccupied this morning."

Drea ignores the question. She glances at the phone and smiles. "Let's see who Chad was really talking to. Can you redial on a pay phone?"

"Negative," Amber says. "But we *could* call the operator and tell them to dial back the last number. We can just say that it's an emergency and we can't remember the last digit or something."

"It'll never work," Drea says. "But let's try it."

Amber picks up the receiver, dials a zero, and waits a few seconds. "Hello? Why aren't you picking up?" She finger-punches the zero a bunch more times before hanging up. "Oh my god, what if this was, like, an emergency or something?"

The phone rings. We look at each other, unsure of what to do, if we should get it. Two rings. Three. Amber's mouth quivers, as though she's about to say something, but instead she picks up the receiver. "Hello? Yes." She covers her free ear to hear better. "What?" She lifts the receiver from her ear, but instead of hanging it up, she passes it to Drea. "It's for you."

Drea crinkles her eyebrows, confused. She takes the phone, and Amber and I huddle in close to listen. "Hello?" Drea says.

There's a long pause before a static-filled voice—his voice—speaks to us. "Sorry I couldn't stick around to chat, Drea. But I'll be sure to call you later when it's more private and we can talk about more intimate things, like your bra."

"My bra?"

"Pink. Lace trim around the cups. Size 34B."

Oh! My! God! I press my eyes shut, jar my mouth, and let a long, audible huff of air spew out my mouth. *He* has my laundry.

Drea dangles the phone in between two fingers and starts to hyperventilate. I take the receiver from her and the voice continues in my ear: "Tell your friends it isn't nice to eavesdrop on other people's phone calls. I don't want to talk to *them*, Drea. I want to talk to you. I want to *be* with you. And soon, that will happen."

The phone clicks on the other end. I drop the receiver so that it dangles inches from the ground.

Amber snatches a notebook out of some freshman's hand and starts fanning Drea's face with it. "Just breathe," Amber says. "Try and catch your breath."

"I can't do this anymore," Drea mumbles between puffs. "I can't. . . ." Her voice trails off in a series of desperate gasps.

"I know." I take her hands and help her to sit down on the cement curbing. "I think maybe you should go home for a week or so, until this is over."

"You should, Drea," Amber says.

Drea shakes her head and swats Amber's notebook-fanning away. "I'll be okay," she says, regaining her breath.

"Are you sure?" I ask. "Do you want to go lie down?"

"I'm fine."

The dial tone plays from the receiver like a horrible reminder that he's still with us somehow.

"He's screwing with us," Amber says.

Drea straightens up a bit. "How did he know we were going to come here? How does he know about my bra?"

Yikes. I didn't want to tell her about the bra or the hanky in the first place, because I didn't want to admit about the pee-stained laundry. I just wanted to put the whole incident behind me and hope it didn't come back.

"How did he know we'd be together?" Drea looks at Amber and me for answers, as if we have them.

"Because he's screwing with us," Amber says. "Whoever is behind this knows all of us pretty well. He knows that I have the pay phone numbers listed in my address book and that's why he didn't block the call."

"And he knew we'd come running out here to find him," I finish.

"I bet he can see us," Amber says, peering around the quad. "He's probably watching us right now. Probably has a cell phone."

"Then why would he use the pay phone?" Drea asks, the color returning to her cheeks.

"To throw us off track," Amber says. "That's what I'd do."

"He's always a step ahead," Drea says.

I draw up on Drea's sweater, pluck the protection bottle from her waist, and place it in her hands. "He may be a step ahead now," I say. "But he won't be for long."

fifteen

It's just past ten o'clock and Drea and I have each taken our stations in bed. Me trying to work through a bunch of word problems for trig, Drea mapping out a Chaucer essay. I tried taking a snooze right after dinner, but I think insomnia has kicked in. I'm hoping the word problems will help do the trick.

It's dead quiet between us. I guess it's an understatement to say we haven't exactly been getting along lately. But it's also an understatement to say we've both had our reasons to go into bitch mode. I almost wish Amber were around to chisel through the ice wall between our beds, but she ended up studying with PJ tonight. It's true what Drea says about the two of them—they really should go out again. But Amber is from the school of "My parents were high school sweethearts and still make out like crazy so I refuse to be in a relationship that isn't as perfect as theirs." I guess we all have our hang-ups.

Personally, I don't know what I'm thinking half the time, flirting with Chad, right in front of Drea. But sometimes I just can't help myself, can't bridle the raging hormones I feel beating through my bones, stirring up my blood.

Sort of a shitty friend-thing to do, I know. But I also know I've been blaming my sour-grapes routine on a serious lack of sleep, when I think it's more like a serious lack of self-confidence.

I glance up at Maura's watercolor picture of us sitting on the porch swing, playing cards. I take a deep breath and stifle the self-pity I feel tearing up in my eyes. Maybe what I need is a good dose of Mom. I grab the phone and call her, but unfortunately she isn't home or isn't picking up, so I leave her a message to call me back.

"Drea," I say, flipping my trig book shut, "do you want to talk?"

"Actually, I do." She comes and sits across from me on the bed. "Look, I know I've been a major bitch lately. Earlier, with Chad, during the whole protection bottle thing, the hockey jersey . . . I'm just totally flipping out here, Stacey, and I don't know what to do."

"I feel like *I've* been the bitch," I say.

"Oh, please," she says, "a little respect here for the Queen B."

Drea and I end up staying up, doing something we haven't done in a very long time: acting normal. We paint our toenails watermelon pink, give each other banana facials, and yogurt-condition each other's hair. We top off all our beautifying with what else but food—our own version of Rice Krispie treats with what's left in the room: cornflakes and peanut butter.

The night is deliciously normal, taking us away for a spell from the horrible reality that sits above us like a black cloud, waiting to pour. But once the food is washed away and the last Krispie treat eaten, the downpour begins and I feel compelled to ask Drea about the guy who's been calling and her relationship with him.

"I just thought it was a wrong number gone right." Drea lays across the end of my bed, her cheek pressed against her paisley pillow, staring off at the wall.

"How often did you talk to him?"

"Not that often. I don't know, maybe five or six times."

"What do you know about him?"

"Not much. Like I said, he didn't want to exchange names. We mostly just talked about situations—you know, like how each other felt about certain things."

"Like what?"

"Like dating stuff." She laughs—a nervous giggle—and rolls over onto her back.

"What kind of dating stuff?"

"You know, the kind of stuff you do on dates."

"You mean s-e-x stuff?"

"Well, yeah. I mean, not all the time, but sometimes." She holds a leg up midair to peek at her watermelon-pink toenails, annoyance growing in her voice. "It wasn't what you're thinking, Stacey. I mean, he was really nice at first. It didn't bother me. It needs to bother the person for it to be considered harassment or something."

Is she crazy? I want to ask her that, want to slap her silly. I mean, what is she thinking? How could she just go on talking to some perv like that, some guy she doesn't even know?

But instead of pointing out every single red flag in their screwed-up little relationship, I listen, trying my best not to judge, biting my tongue at all the serious deviations in common sense: questions about petting versus grinding, about what each of them was wearing at the time of the conversation. And my own personal favorite: him starting to refer to them as a couple, getting all jealous when Drea wasn't around to answer his calls, and Drea going along with it.

Drea relays all of this information in no more than five seconds, her eyes focused up at the ceiling, like she's embarrassed by it all. And I'm trying to respect her, doing my best not to show even a single speck of horror on my face, nodding in all the right places. But she's looking at me now, lips scrunched up like she wants to be sick, and so I feel compelled to ask:

"What's wrong?"

"I told him about, you know, how far I've gone."

"What do you mean, *how far?*"

"*Stacey?!*" She rolls her eyes. "I mean how *far* . . . how far around *the bases.*"

Oh.

"I told him how me and Chad flew through second, made it to third, started for home run, but then got struck out."

Drea must sense my confusion because she rolls her eyes for the second time this evening and blurts, "We *struck out*, Stacey! We were all ready to do it, had all the supplies we needed, but then I guess I sort of freaked, and so we decided not to."

She makes it sound like some camping trip. Still, I'm not sure I want to be hearing any of this, but I listen anyway. We talk about their conversations for a good hour. And at the end of it Drea seems, oddly enough, more relaxed, less jittery, I think, because I haven't said much more than *uh huh* and *em hmm* the whole time. But now my somewhat-silence is bugging her because she's propped herself up on her elbows, awaiting my response.

"So?" she asks.

"So what?" I answer, trying to erase the mental images now planted in my brain of my best friend and love object *almost* home-running. "What do you want me to say?"

"Do you think I was wrong?"

"I don't think it's a question of right or wrong, Drea." A big fat lie. "I think you probably did what you felt was comfortable for you at the time."

"Well, it was kind of wrong," Drea says. "I mean, now that I think about it, I must have been completely nuts."

An understatement.

"I mean, he could be some crazy psycho pedophile ax-murderer for all I know," she continues.

"Em hmm."

"That's why I don't want to tell my parents about it, or anyone. I just feel so dumb. I really thought he—you know, cared about me. It was kind of nice."

I give Drea a hug and twist my fingers through her hair, catching a bit of yogurt residue on my finger. "You're not dumb."

"It was just because, I don't know, he was nice and you weren't around that first time he called, and I had just gotten off the phone with my mom, and she told me all this stuff about how I might be spending next summer with just her at Grampy's house, and I don't know, it was just . . . easy."

"I know about slipping into easy," I say. "Sometimes it fits pretty nice."

"Plus, that first time he called, I kind of thought it was Chad, but now I don't know. I mean, I think I'd be able to tell Chad's voice after all this time."

"Maybe, like you said, it's more than one person. Or maybe whoever it is is using one of those voice changer thingies."

"Do *you* think it's Chad?" Drea asks.

"I don't know. I don't want to think it's him, but it sort of makes sense, especially since he had the jersey. I definitely think it's someone on campus. Someone our age who knows everybody, who knows the workings of this place."

"Who?"

"I don't know," I say. "But we're gonna find out."

After I've given her a full French braid, Drea returns to her bed and snuggles up for sleep. That's when the phone rings.

I pick it up. "Hello?"

"Hi, Stacey. I got your message. I hope I'm not calling too late." It's my mother. I sink back into the comfort of my covers, just hearing her voice, a little piece of home.

"No, Mom," I say. "This is a perfect time."

sixteen

After my short stint of normalcy with Drea, and a surprisingly pleasant phone conversation with Mom, I fasten the silver dream necklace around my neck, fall asleep pretty easily, and don't wake up until morning.

Except I don't have a nightmare, don't remember any of my dreams, and am starting to feel like a complete and utter failure.

While Drea and Amber go off to classes, I call the school secretary, feigning stomach cramps, and wallow in the misery of my bed. I try to get myself to fall back asleep. I light incense, count stars, and start a dream journal, but nothing works. I'm so completely awake I want to throw up. This is how I spend my entire day. Stacey Brown, Sleep Loser. Stacey Brown, who ditches school and can't even enjoy the playing-hooky basics of sleeping in.

Drea and Amber come straight to the room after classes and I confess to them my failures.

"Bummer," Amber says.

I'm starting to feel even less confident than I did before, and that's what prompts the next couple hours. I try to convince Drea to go to campus police, to tell them about everything that's been going on.

Finally, after much sweat shed from Amber and I, Drea agrees and she and Amber head off to talk to them. I, on the verge of pulling out each of my hairs, one by one, offer to join them, but Drea wants me to stay in bed and try to catch some snooze.

Joy.

Just barely six o'clock in the evening, it already looks like well past nine outside. I decide to take an herbal sponge-bath in the sink in our room, hoping the blending of water and flowers will help do the trick.

Gram used to swear to taking baths before spells and before bed. Baths, not showers. There is a difference, according to her. She said the body needs to be purified in preparation for that which is sacred, that the senses don't work to their fullest when the energy hasn't been cleansed. Of course, it's hard to take a bath when your school only has stand-up showers. Especially when those stand-up showers can only handle two inches of water when the drain is blocked before water starts spilling out onto the floor.

I plug the drain with the stopper and fill up the sink to three-quarters of the way full with lukewarm water. It's one of those old-fashioned sinks—white porcelain with silver fixtures—attached to the wall on my side of the room. To the water, I add the carnation petals from the flower I borrowed out of the vase in the dorm lobby. Then I add in droplets of rosemary, peppermint, and patchouli oils, and a handful of mint leaves—all soothing, clarifying herbs and flowers that will hopefully help me sleep long and soundly and, most importantly, will help make my dreams more insightful.

I unscrew the cap off the bottle of talcum powder and sift a tablespoonful into a ceramic cup. To it, I add four tablespoons of honey and stir. The talcum powder will help clarify images in my dreams that might confuse me, while the honey will help my dreams stick in place, so I can remember. I spoon the mixture into the sink with a finger and then mix the stew of water with my hand, encouraging all the ingredients to blend and intensify.

I lay a towel on the floor for spillage, change into my red and ratty terrycloth robe—a favorite in my growing collection of comfort clothing—and dip a sea-sponge into the water. Leaving my robe open, I begin with my legs, sponging down the length, breathing in the floral vapors as I reach down to my feet. "Oils and water, flower and herb, give me vision, give me sight on my walk this night." I repeat the chant three times aloud, imagining the sea of oils mixing and purifying my skin and the air I breathe. I redip the sponge and move up to my belly, then up a bit more to my neck and shoulders. I close my eyes and concentrate on the nature CD I fed into Drea's player—trickling water seasoned with just the right amount of birdsong. It's the last ingredient to a recipe that will help tranquilize my spirit so that I can experience insightful dreams, ones that aren't blocked by my own fears.

I know why my dreams haven't been so telling these past couple days. Gram used to say that in order to have insightful dreams, you need to be brave enough to accept the consequences. At the time she told me this, sitting across from her over tea, playing gin rummy and eating butter biscuits, I didn't really understand what she meant, but now it makes perfect sense.

I know I haven't been brave about dreaming. I know my subconscious side is probably picking up on the fact that I'm scared to death. A part of me died inside when I failed Maura. I can't fail again because if I do, what remains of me will die as well. And then there'll be nothing left.

I glide the sponge over my face, concentrating on the idea of strength, imagining the water washing away any trace of fear. The exercise empowers me, restores the energy I've been missing. I glance down at my amethyst ring and kiss the stone, imagining Gram's cheek, fully believing that, in some way, she's here with me.

I wrap myself up in the robe and move over to my night table. I reach inside the drawer for a yellow wax crayon and a note pad. I need to think of a question I can ask my dream.

Something clever. Something that might reveal the truth in more than one way. But the only question I end up scribbling down is the one that seems most obvious: WHO IS AFTER DREA?

I fold it up, slip it inside the dream bag, and deposit it into my pillowcase. Then I crawl into bed, close my eyes, and imagine warm teabags sitting atop the lids. With each breath, I picture the waning moon, growing more narrow and shallow, until it's no more than a speck of light.

Just about to travel off to sleep, I hear a knock at the corner window. "Stacey," calls a voice through the glass.

Chad.

"Come on, Stace," he says. "Let me in."

I get up from the bed, tighten the belt on my robe, and head over to the window. That's when I'm reminded— when my annoyance at his incredible knack for dropping by at the most awkward times dissolves. He looks amazing. While he looks off into the night, waiting for me to let him in, I study the way his black leather jacket hugs around his shoulders, the way his hair is messed up to perfection. How he's wearing wire-rimmed glasses instead of his usual contacts.

I, on the other hand, can feel a glob of talcum powder caked in my hair, a smidgen of honey against my neck. But I'm still on a makeover high from last night, and after the sponge bath, I'm feeling surprisingly sexy.

He looks up at me when he hears the lock unlatch, and I watch a smile grow on his cheek. It's a knowing smile, a confident one. A smile that tells me he knows what I'm thinking, and he feels the same.

I tug up on the window and pull a stool over to sit, so we can talk at eye-level.

"Hi." He lifts the window even wider and leans his elbows onto the sill. He's chewing gum, a skinny, mint-colored piece that flips back and forth over his tongue.

"Hi." I swallow hard and watch his eyes notice the movement in my throat.

"Did I disturb you?"

"No," I say. "I just took a sponge bath."

"Really?" he says. "Maybe I should have come sooner."

A nervous giggle spatters out my mouth, making a weird gurgling sound. But Chad's expression remains serious, as though he really means it.

"So, are you alone?"

I squeeze my legs together, feeling the urge to pee. "For a little while."

"Good. I wanted to talk to you." He leans his body closer, and I can smell the mint of his gum.

"About what?"

"About us." His eyes linger at my neck, the way I've allowed the vee of my robe to open up.

I shift to sit on the heel of my foot in an effort to stop the tugging urge to pee. "What about us?" I clench my teeth and swallow down the pain.

He plucks a folded piece of paper from his back pocket. It has my name, written in red block lettering across the front, the same lettering as in the other notes. "This one is for you."

"Are you the one who's been sending these?"

"Would that bother you?"

"What do you mean? Are you—"

"I mean, would you still like me if I were the one?" Chad moves his face so close that I can feel the heat of his mouth, moistening mine. This is so wrong. I can't like him.

"Yes, you can," he says, as though reading my mind.

My mouth twitches, anticipating the minty flavor of his kiss. I try to distract myself by looking everywhere else—his forehead, his nose, his right earlobe—but my eyes can't help but land back on those lips—slim, pale pink, sculptured to fit my mouth. I hold my eyes closed in a prolonged blink, waiting for him to touch me with those lips.

"Open the note first," he breathes.

The area below my stomach stings with pressure. "Chad," I say. "I have to go to the bathr—"

"Just open it," he says. "It's what you've been waiting for."

I take a deep breath and unfold the note, the message printed across the middle: LOVE IS FUNNY.

"Love is funny?" I question.

"I guess if you think about it," he says. "*Everything* is funny for some people." He touches my face with a brush of his hand, sending electrifying tingles straight down to my watermelon-pink toenails. "Wait," he says, as if just remembering, "I have something else." He pulls three lilies from behind his back and hands them to me. "Be sure to give these to Drea."

"I don't understand," I say.

"You will." He leans forward and places his mouth on mine, his kiss exploding across my lips and at the tip of my tongue.

Behind us, I hear keys jingling against the door. There are voices too—mingling together, whispering. Someone's coming, but I can't move myself away.

Nor do I want to.

The door squeaks open and Chad is still kissing me. A set of shoes clunks their way across the wooden floor, stopping just behind me.

"Stacey?" says Drea's voice.

But I can't steal myself away. I won't.

"Stacey!" she repeats. "Wake up. Wake *up*!"

I feel my body being shaken, and when I finally do wake up, Drea and Amber are hovering over my bed.

"Did you have another nightmare?" Drea asks.

"Um . . ." My head is spinning; it just felt so real. "I don't know. Give me a minute."

"You were breathing all weird," she says. "Practically hyperventilating."

I shift in bed and feel a slight dampness in my pants. Lovely. "I have to go to the bathroom." I pull the comforter over the sheet and do my best to walk backwards, as nonchalantly as can be possible, out the door and down the hallway.

Lucky for me, the shower room is empty. I pull at the back of my robe to check for leakage. It's only a little wet and you can't really tell that much through the dark terrycloth fabric. I squirt some dispenser soap into my palm, peel the robe off, and jump into the shower, doing my best not to get my hair too wet so Drea and Amber won't notice.

All the while I'm scrubbing, I'm trying to focus on the dream and what it means, but I can't stop thinking about the kiss. *That kiss!* I place my fingers over my lips and can feel them tingle, like he's still lingering there. "Love is funny," I whisper into the water. I want to figure out the meaning of love, of each word he said, of mint-flavored chewing gum. Anything to keep my mind distracted from the biggest question of all—why my dreams brought Chad to the window.

I step out of the shower, slip back into my robe, and join Drea and Amber back in the room.

"Bad nacho dip," I say, patting my stomach. But they're not even listening. Amber is checking out Drea's CD collection and Drea is on the phone with her mom. I sit on the edge of my bed, peel my robe off, and fish a fresh T-shirt and pair of boxers from the recyclable clothing pile on the floor.

"Drea's music is so out," Amber says. "And what's with this nature crap?" Her voice is followed by a knocking against the window.

It's PJ. I know because his knock is always the same, a series of thumps that he claims raps out to the tune of *I Dream of Jeannie.*

"Oops. I guess we forgot about him," Amber says. "Wanna let him in, Stace?"

I pull up on the window shade and look down. PJ's circular patch of highlighter-yellow hair stares up at me in the moonlight. "You dyed your hair again," I say, letting him in.

"Blondes have more fun," he says.

"Looks more like booger-yellow to me," Amber says.

"Don't even talk to me. I could have popsicled out there. I think parts of me probably already did."

"Thanks for that visual," Amber says.

PJ moves to the once-broken window and starts examining the borders. "I see you got the window fixed." He flips the lock back and forth. "You gals must have an in with maintenance. It took them two weeks before they came to fix our toilet."

"That's because you're full of shit," Amber says.

"Speaking of," PJ says. "What are you cooking up in here, Stace? Eau de excrement?"

"Very funny," I say, and as soon as I say it, I think about the note in my dream and what it said, how Chad said some people think everything is funny.

Drea hangs up the phone and scoots toward the edge of her bed. "So," she begins, "going to campus police was a complete waste of time."

"How so?" I kick my robe under the bed and drag an extra blanket over the pee spot.

"You can probably guess. They made a report, told us we were probably overreacting, but to be on the safe side, they'll have an extra cruiser around our room at night."

"Looks like we'll miss your midnight visits, PJ," I say.

"Won't stop me," he says. "Somebody's gotta protect you gals at night."

"Oh yeah. I feel safe." Amber makes the sign of the cross.

"Security said they really can't do anything until something significant happens," Drea says.

"Like what?" I ask.

"Like someone croaks," Amber says. "Then they'll take us seriously."

I look at PJ, whose expression doesn't show one iota of confusion. "PJ," I say, "do you have any idea what we're talking about?"

"I guess we kind of filled him in on stuff," Amber says.

"Just PJ?"

"Well, Chad too," she says. "But that's it."

"Great," I say. "Now everyone's gonna know. What happened to our pact?"

"I'm thinking about going home," Drea says. "Just for a semester. I sort of brought it up with my mother just now. I told her I'm not doing well this term and don't want to ruin my GPA. I can always make it up in summer school."

"Is she okay with that?" I ask.

She shrugs. "I guess she and my dad are kind of fighting a lot."

"They need to hang out with my horn-dog parents for a little while," Amber says.

"Oh yeah?" PJ says, turning to Amber. "Maybe you and I should take example from your parentals."

"Not even a chance," Amber says.

"You didn't say that last year."

"Last year was different." She stands in the mirror, penciling blue hearts on both cheeks with a lip liner. "I was so immature."

"So, PJ, to what do we owe such non-pleasure?" I ask.

He pounces down beside me on the bed. "*Nada, mademoiselle.*"

"No wonder he's failing French," Drea says.

PJ blows her an air kiss and then continues to talk in my ear, his guacamole breath making me want to puke. "I was just walking these lovely ladies back to their dorm, and wanted to come and wish my good friend Stacey good night. *C'est tout.*"

"And?" I ask.

"Just tell her," Drea says. "She needs to know."

"All in good time, love dove." He crosses his legs at the knee and kicks a foot back and forth. "So, Stace, what's all this I hear about some crazy stalker and how you're going to stop him? I want juice."

"PJ, I really don't feel like—"

"*Très intéressant, mademoiselle.*" PJ taps a finger over his mouth in thought. "So BVS of you."

"BVS?"

"Hel-looo?" He snaps his fingers back and forth over his head, home-girl style. "Buffy, the Vampire Slayer?"

"Of course," I say. "PJ, I'm tired. I want to go to sleep. Tell me what you're going to tell me or—"

"Or what? You'll turn me into a frog?" He wiggles his fingers in front of my face all hocus-pocuslike. *So* obnoxious.

"Why not?" Amber says. "You kiss like one."

"Well, if you were to loan me, say, two nights' worth of French homework, I might be more convinced."

"Just tell her," Amber says. "Or I'll mess up your hair."

"No way, girlfriend. You know how long it takes me to get this look?" PJ runs his fingers over the yellow spikes. "Okay, fine. I'll tell you. Today, after French, I heard Veronica Leeman, a.k.a. Snotty Ronnie, say that she's been getting some weird phone calls."

"What kind of calls?"

"Your typical stalker—hang ups, heavy breathing, some perv who says he wants her."

"Did she go to campus security?" I ask.

"I don't know," PJ says. "Maybe. She was pretty psycho about it."

"She's psycho anyway," Drea says.

"You just don't like her because she's got the hots for Chad," Amber says.

"Wait," I say, "what did you hear her say exactly?"

"That'll cost you two nights' worth of French homework."

"I suck at French. You know that."

"Gotta fill the pages with something."

"Fine." I point to my French workbook in the corner.

"Okay, what was yesterday's homework?" PJ flips through the pages.

"Page fifty-three to fifty-five, exercises A, B, C, F, and H."

He checks those exercises before tossing the book back into the corner.

"Anyway," Amber says.

"Anyway," he repeats, "so, I was standing in the hallway and, you know, Snotty Ronnie was combing that nest she has on her head . . . . " PJ surveys around the room as he talks, checking out the knickknacks on Drea's bureau. He stops mid-sentence at Drea's teardrop earrings. *"Très chic,* Dray. Must borrow."

"Do I have to take my homework back?" I ask.

"Très rude, mademoiselle. Is that the way you treat all your guests?" He uncaps Drea's antiperspirant bottle and sniffs. "So, anyway. I'm just walking along, pretending to mind

my own business, when I hear Snotty Ronnie telling a bunch of her snotty friends that she's been getting these prank calls."

"What do they say to her?" Drea asks.

PJ rolls the antiperspirant ball at the front and sides of his neck. "Something about coming after her and ripping off all her clothes."

Drea bites down on one of her acrylic nails, causing what she would normally deem an emergency repair, but she's so sucked into the moment, she doesn't even notice.

"You're serious?" she asks.

"No. Who'd want to see her in the buff? Can anyone say Grinch alert?"

"Duh, the Grinch is a guy," Amber says.

"Precisely," he says.

"Come on, PJ, be serious," Amber says.

"For a kiss."

"Kiss this." Amber points her butt in his direction.

"Don't tempt me, kitten," he says. "So anyway, all these pranks, wanting to sex her up, yada yada ya, and—"

"What?" Drea asks.

"The juiciest—apparently he can see her when he calls."

"How does she know he's watching?" Drea tightens the neck of her blouse.

"Because," PJ's voice dwarfs into spooky mode, "he knows what she's wearing and who she's with. He even knew when she reached into her bag and took out . . . " PJ pauses for effect.

"*What?*" Drea asks. "Took out *what?*"

"When she took out a metal garden rake to comb through that hair." He grabs at his stomach and starts laughing, like the complete idiot that he really is.

None of us join him.

"I think you better leave, funny boy," Amber says.

"Come on," he says. "Where's your sense of humor?"

I move to sit beside Drea, allowing her head to fall against my shoulder. She holds her hands over her throat and tries to calm her breathing.

"Drea," PJ says. "It was a joke. I'm sorry."

"I think you better leave," I say.

Amber yanks at his arm, trying to lead him back over to the window.

"Fine. I'll go," he says, pulling away from her. "I don't need to be told twice."

"Yes, you do," Amber says.

"Sorry, puppet," he says to Drea. "I guess I can get carried away sometimes. Scratch what I said about the rake, but everything else is legit. Friends?" He extends his hand for a shake, but Drea ignores it. "Fine, leave me hanging." He runs the hand over his hair spikes. "I'll let myself out."

Amber closes the window behind him and flips the lock shut. "He can be such a boy."

"It's not his fault," Drea says. "He's just being PJ. It's whoever's doing this."

"We need to talk to Veronica Leeman," Amber says, flipping her nose in the air.

"She'll never talk to us." Drea grabs the protection bottle and holds it close.

"She has to," I say. "But first, I've been thinking about trying something new."

"Drugs or girls?" Amber asks.

"Very funny." I unlatch the silver dream necklace from around my neck, and dangle the crystal I added to it in front of their eyes.

"I can't be hypnotized," Amber says. "I've tried it on myself before. Doesn't work."

"I'm not trying to hypnotize you. I just want you to look at it. My grandmother gave this crystal to me. She told me that with it, I'd always be able to know she was watching."

"No offense, Stace, but it's just a crystal. You can buy them anywhere. I have a green one back in my room. I wear it with my grasshopper earrings."

"No," I say, rubbing my thumb over the grooves, "this one's different. It's a Devic crystal. See the fractures and chunks? For every chip, there's insight and spirit."

"What does Devic mean?" Drea asks.

"It means communication with the spirits in nature. It means opening our hearts to the magic of nature and Mother Earth."

"Spirits?" Drea asks.

"I've been thinking about conducting a séance."

"You're serious?"

"Completely. I think my grandmother can help us with this. But I need your help, too. Both of you."

"I'm so in," Amber says.

"I don't know." Drea chews off the remainder of her nail tip. "Is it dangerous? I mean, can it make things worse or kill somebody or something?"

"Not if we do it right," I say. "Just think about it, okay? But first, let's go find Veronica Leeman."

seventeen

We decide to track Veronica Leeman down in the campus café, since that's where she normally hangs out. On the way there, I end up telling Drea and Amber the G-rated version of my nightmare.

I tell them how Chad showed up at the window, about the love-is-funny note, and how he gave me three lilies to pass on to Drea. Three lilies—not four—probably to denote that a day has passed, that we're just one day closer to whatever impending danger awaits us. Amber asks me all sorts of questions—did Chad mention PJ's name, was he laughing when he gave me the lilies or was he all somber about it—but all Drea can ask me is why I was dreaming about Chad in the first place.

I take a deep breath, silently count to five, and tell her that Chad's appearance in my dream is probably insignificant. That I may have dreamt about him because he came to the window yesterday with that note from his hockey jersey.

Or maybe it's because he really does have something to do with all this.

We swing the door of the campus café open and there's Veronica, sitting at a ring-shaped table with Donna Tillings, the class gossip. We don't normally hang out here since it's not really our crowd—popular cliques mixed with tormented-artist types. The café used to be a theater way back, before they started using the auditorium for plays, so they still keep the whole drama motif going—stage and audience seating, script-style menus, and director's chairs. Teachers and administrators call the café by its name, On Stage, but everyone else calls it Hangman, coined because legend has it some girl hanged herself here when she didn't get the starring role in *Carousel*.

"I so love the smell of coffee," Amber says. "I'm gonna get one." She leans over the counter and notices Donovan sitting in the corner, sipping an espresso and sketching the cream and sugar station. "Hi, Donovan," Amber sings, peeking at Drea. "Wanna buy me a coffee?" Donovan waves, but quickly returns to his work.

"I guess that's a no," Drea says. "Besides, don't you know that coffee makes your teeth brown?" Drea eyes the trays of goodies behind the glass counter—cinnamon scones, chocolate chip and Macadamia nut cookies, pink frosted gingerbread men with pink nooses tied around the necks. "Did you guys forget why we're here?" I ask.

"No," Drea says. "Let's get this over with. Veronica Lee-man is not exactly my favorite person to talk to."

"Look," I say, "you guys may have something significant in common. You need to at least try to get along with her for the next ten minutes."

"I know exactly what we have in common. She's been after my boyfriend for as long as I've known her."

"Hate to burst your bubble, Dray, but he's not exactly yours anymore." Amber eyes Donna Tillings, stirring up a café mocha with whipped cream. "Yummy. May it go straight to her thighs and plant years of cellulite. Stacey, work your magic."

"Are you kidding?" Drea says. "Donna's thighs are already control-top material."

"So right," Amber says, taking a second look.

"Can you guys just stop?" I say. "We're here to talk to Veronica."

"Snotty Ronnie," Amber corrects.

I glance at Veronica. She's sipping coffee from a cereal bowl, the way they do it in France, according to our French textbook. She looks up at me, mid-sip, and then whispers something in Donna's ear. Donna laughs. She clinks her overflowing mug against Veronica's bowl to toast their joke.

"I can't stomach them," Amber says. "Let's bug."

"We can't," I say. "Not yet."

Veronica whispers something else to Donna before scooting out from the table.

"She's coming over here," Drea says.

"Snot alert." Amber shoots her nose in the air.

"You guys have a problem?" Veronica asks. "You look a little out of place."

"The only thing out of place is your hair," Amber says. "Anybody got a match?"

"Ha ha." Veronica nonchalantly pats the hairspray-glued clump piled high on her head.

"Don't listen to her," Drea says, evil-eyeing Amber. "She can be so immature sometimes."

Veronica looks Drea up and down, stopping a moment to raise an eyebrow at the length of her plaid skirt, the way Drea has shortened it by rolling the waist. "It's a shame we haven't been able to chat much this year," Veronica tells her. "Maybe if I spent more time around the boys' dorm we'd bump into each other. But then again, I don't want to get a rep. You know what that can do."

I take a step between them. "Actually, Veronica, we were looking for you."

"Really?" she says.

"Hard to believe, isn't it?" Amber douses her palm with the cinnamon shaker and licks at the sprinkles.

I elbow her to shut up.

"You know, Stacey," Veronica begins, "you really freaked me out in French class the other day when you fell asleep. It's not every day you hear someone just start screaming that they killed some girl. Let alone in French class."

"I said I *didn't* kill her."

"Whatever. What's all that about? Everyone's been buzzing."

"First answer my question," I say.

"Why should I?"

"Because I know you cheated on the French exam and I can prove it," I say. "Cheating's against the Honor Code. Grounds for suspension."

Amber pauses mid-lick across her palm and Drea's mouth drops open. I bite down on the skin of my tongue, waiting for Veronica to challenge my bluff.

"Fine," Veronica says, after a pause. "What do you want to know?"

I motion to an empty table against the wall and we sit, me and Drea on one side, Amber and Veronica on the other.

"So?" Veronica says. "What's this all about?"

"We heard you've been getting some pranks lately," I say.

"Who told you that?"

"Everyone's been buzzing," Amber mimics.

I kick Amber under the table.

"Do you know who it is?" Drea asks.

Veronica shakes her head and looks away. "It's been three nights in a row now."

"What kind of phone calls?" I ask.

Veronica shrugs. "He tries to talk to me. The first time he called, he was, like, 'guess who this is.'"

"Has it only been phone calls?" I ask.

"The first two nights, phone calls." Veronica takes in a deep breath.

"Then?" Drea props her elbows on the table to lean in closer. "You can trust us."

"Why should I believe that?"

"Because it's been happening to me too," Drea says. "I think it might be the same person."

Veronica looks at Drea, as though seeing her for the first time. "Are you scared?"

"I've been nothing but scared. I feel like I'm being watched, like I can't even go to the cafeteria or take a shower."

"I know what you mean," Veronica says. "I don't feel safe here."

"I've actually been thinking about leaving for a while." Drea snatches a chocolate shaker from Amber, sprinkles a handful of the powder into her palm, and uses what's left of a nail tip to spoon it onto her tongue.

Veronica settles back into her chair, a bit more at ease talking to us. "So, has it only been prank phone calls for you?"

Drea looks at me, I think, wishing I'd grant her some blessing that it's okay to tell Veronica everything. But I can't. I won't. Because I simply don't know if it is okay.

"No," Drea says. "It started out that way, but then he sent me this gift, along with a note."

Veronica's face blanches; her aura turns a sour green. "He did the same for me. Last night. It was waiting in the hallway outside my room when I got home."

"What was inside?" Drea asks.

I watch the two of them exchange anguish while Amber remains oblivious, concocting some spice recipe in her hand. It's like what they say about tragedy bringing people closer, even the worst of enemies. It's the first time I've ever seen Veronica Leeman look scared.

"Flowers," Veronica says. She glances down at her hands to check for shaking.

"Lilies?" Drea asks.

"Yeah. How did you know?"

"How many?" Drea clasps her hands over Veronica's.

"Three," she says. "Three lilies. For the number of days until he comes for me."

eighteen

After our chat with Veronica at the Hangman Café, I come back to the dorm for some sleep. But what I really end up doing is tossing and turning in bed; flipping and flopping, tugging the covers up over my ears to no avail. It's just so weird being alone in the room for more than fifteen minutes. So weird without Drea, tossing and turning right along with me.

After she and Veronica spilled guts over frothy cappuccino and fresh biscotti—about the flowers and the notes and the whole stalker fiasco—Drea declared she needed a night off campus and called her aunt, who lives two towns away, to come and pick her up. I suggested that she just spend the entire weekend there, until her D-day passes, but Drea flat out rejected. Now that she and Veronica have bonded, Drea is committed to helping her out. Talking to Veronica, I think, just made everything seem so real for Drea.

So why do I feel like Veronica's such a fake?

It just doesn't make sense to me. It doesn't make sense that the same person would go after Drea *and* Veronica. The two of them couldn't be more different. And don't stalkers usually go for the same type of person? Regardless, Drea is staying at her aunt's until sometime tomorrow afternoon, and then we're all supposed to get together to come up with a plan.

I roll over in bed, try squashing a pillow under my knees, and even drag my history book under the covers to see if that will put me to sleep. No luck. There's no way I'm falling asleep, at least not until Drea calls as promised.

"Love is funny," I say, trying to take my mind off the phone. I repeat the cryptic phrase over and over again, as though repetition of the words will make sense of them somehow. For me, love hasn't exactly been a comedy lately, more like a downright tragedy, but there has to be a clue in there somewhere.

I roll myself out of bed to fetch the thick purple candle I used during Drea's card reading. I light it for inspiration and insight and watch the shallow bowl that surrounds the wick fill up with hot liquid wax.

The phone rings. I jump to answer it. "Hello? Drea?"

"This isn't Drea," says the male voice on the other end. "And I know she isn't home. It's you, Stacey. I want to talk to you."

My hands shake just hearing his voice, just hearing him say my name. *Him.*

"I know you're alone tonight, Stacey," he continues. "That's why I called. Aren't you gonna ask me how I'm doing?"

"What do you want?"

"I told you already. I want to talk to you."

"I'm not alone," I say, looking down at my amethyst.

He laughs—slow and deliberate. "Why are you lying, Stacey? I know you're alone. All night. Just you and your candles."

I click the phone off, yank both window shades down to the sills, and check and double-check the door to make sure it's locked.

My heart pummels inside my chest, like something's trying to get out. I pluck the baseball bat from behind the door and sit, perched in the middle of my bed, ready and waiting for I have no idea what.

The phone rings again. I don't want to answer it, but I have to. It might be Drea. And I can't run away.

I'm just about to pick it up when it stops. I snatch it up anyway to call Amber. I know she won't mind staying over with me or, better yet, I could go there. I start to press at the numbers, but it isn't dialing. "Hello?" I say into the receiver.

"Why did you hang up on me?" he asks.

It's him. Again. My chin shakes. My heart pounds. My fingers turn bloodless, strengthless, causing me to almost drop the phone.

But then his voice, again, seething in my ear: "I asked you a question," he says.

"Who is this?"

"You'll all know soon enough."

"What do you want from me?" I squeeze the Devic crystal between my fingers, hoping its energy will soak through my pores and grant me the strength I need.

"A little bird told me that you were some freak in a carnival," he says, after a pause.

"*What?*" I ask.

"I heard that you can see things in your dreams, like some psychic or something."

"What kinds of things?"

"Things about me and Drea," he says. "Stuff that might ruin my surprise for her."

"What surprise?"

"If you were a real witch, you'd know. Are you?"

"Yes." I feel confident saying this, like the very affirmation is power in itself.

"Stay away from her," he says. "This has nothing to do with you or your so-called witchcraft."

"*You* stay away."

"Don't even try to fuck with me," he says. "Don't forget who's in control here."

"I haven't," I say, challenging him.

"Either you find a way to stay away from her, or *I* will find one for you."

I feel my face turn red, the blood pumping through my veins, high into my cheeks. "What are you going to do to her in three days?" I blurt.

"It wouldn't be a surprise if I told you, now, would it? Oh, and by the way, I'm returning a little gift I found of yours in the laundry room. Seems you've been having a problem lately. Imagine what everyone would say if they found out, Stacey. What do you think Chad would say?"

"Who is this?" I feel myself stand up.

"You mind your own business and I'll mind mine. Sleep tight, Stacey."

There's a click on the other end of the phone when he hangs up. Still, I keep the receiver pressed against my ear, waiting for him to pick up again, waiting for him to tell me how he knows the way I feel about Chad. The phone clicks again, followed by a dial tone.

I drop the receiver and look toward the window. I know what's out there, waiting for me.

I walk over and peek out from behind the shade, toward the lawn. No one. I unlock the pane, pull the window up, and look down.

There it is. The dirty laundry I left in the washroom. The soiled blue sweatpants lay folded on the window ledge under one of the pee-stained sheets. The rest is in a heap on the ground. Still dirty. Still rude and smelly. Still, I burrow my face into a corner of the sheet and allow myself to cry.

nineteen

I scrub the soiled sheets in the sink, the bubbles of white cloth sending puddles of foamy water over the porcelain rim. I try to calm myself, to concentrate on the lapping of the water and its ability to cleanse. To focus on what's really important—saving Drea. But I can't help feeling sorry for myself. His phone call just made me feel so defenseless.

It's one thing when people think you're a freak because you practice Wicca, but it's a completely different story when you're sixteen years old and wetting the bed.

The phone rings. My first thought is that it's Drea. Finally. Calling from her aunt's. I dive into the heap of covers on my bed to answer it. "Hello? Drea?"

"Not last time I checked," says the male voice on the other end.

Like a reflex, I click the phone off. Why is he doing this to me? Why does he keep calling me? I take a deep breath and wait for the phone to ring again. I know it will. And it does. Only this time I'm more prepared. I pick the receiver up and wait for him to speak.

"Stacey?"

Chad? "*Chad?*"

"Yeah, it's me. Why did you hang up before?"

"Oh, I thought . . . ."

"What?"

"Nothing."

"What? That I was that wacko who keeps bothering you guys?"

"Oh yeah," I say. "I forgot Amber told you."

"Not just me. Everybody's talking about it."

"Are you serious, *everybody?*"

"Well, some people."

Note to self: kill Amber. Though maybe it's Veronica who blabbed. It has been a whopping two whole hours since we all said goodbye at the Hangman. A totally doable task for someone with a mouth as big as hers.

"Look," I say, feeling a sudden bout of bitchiness come over me. "Drea isn't here, if that's why you're calling."

"What? I can't just call *you?*"

I jar my mouth, hoping the words will filter down from my brain, but I have no idea what to say, if he's even serious.

"Where is she?" he asks.

"She's staying at her aunt's house tonight." And as soon as I let these word-crumbs dribble out my mouth, I want to eat them back up. He doesn't need to know where Drea is tonight. No one does.

"How come?"

"Why are you calling now? It's almost one."

"I know," he says. "It's just that I couldn't sleep and I've been up all night thinking about how I'm going to fail the physics exam tomorrow. I was hoping you'd still be up, pulling one of your notorious all-nighters."

Physics exam?

"I'm up," I say, finally, "because some sicko likes to call girls in the middle of the night and freak them out. I think I'll call Amber and force her to be up with me."

"I could come by," he says. "I mean, since we both can't sleep and all. No sense bothering Amber. Besides, maybe you could quiz me for the test."

I smooth a hand over the back of my hair and stand up to look in the mirror. "Do you think that's a good idea? I mean—"

"Well, you did say Drea wasn't coming home tonight, right?"

"Yeah?"

"And you're getting all these prank calls. You shouldn't be there by yourself."

I swipe the bangs out of my eyes and chew at my lip. I have no idea what to say to him. Am I supposed to wait another three years to see if things work out between him and Drea, or is it time to take charge of my own fate? I dull the horns and pointy tail I feel I'm beginning to sprout by reminding myself that Chad is my friend too. Why should I feel guilty every time he walks into a room?

"Well?" he says. "Say something."

"Okay. But just to study."

"What else?" he asks, a smile in his voice. "I'll be over in a few."

I hang up before either of us has the chance to say good-bye or change our minds. And as much as I remind myself that this isn't a social call but a chance to cram for physics, I decide dark and baggy sweats are probably not a good look. Instead, I slip into a pair of pink and white pajama bottoms, compliments of Drea's dresser, and a white tank top that's mine. I drain the sink, wring out the sheets, and stuff them into a fresh laundry bag.

Less than fifteen minutes later, Chad is knocking at the window. I unlock it to let him in, then whisk over to sit on my bed, purposely cluttered with physics notes, lab reports, and old quizzes—zero space for him and therefore zero temptation for me.

"You've been busy," he says, shutting the window back up. He glances around my bed for someplace to sit. But the only vacant spots are on the floor, in between clothing piles, or on Drea's bed.

"So, how long have you been studying?" he asks, opting for Drea's bed.

I pretend to be engrossed in the notes from last week's lecture on velocity and mass. "Not long enough," I say, peeking up at him. I can't help it. He just looks so completely perfect. A baseball cap, like he just crawled out of bed. A cuddly cotton sweatshirt that I could just wrap myself up in. Tiny black wire-rimmed glasses. He smiles at me and I can't help but stare at his mouth. Those lips. His teeth. The way the bottom teeth overlap in the front when you look just close enough. I shake my stare away and focus down on my notes. "I guess you could say my grades have sort of taken a dive in the dunk tank this quarter."

"Ditto." He pulls a stack of mangled papers from the inside covers of his textbook and adds it to the collection I've got going on my bed. "What chapter is the test on?"

"Seven. I think."

He readjusts his baseball cap, sending a curl of his scent just under my nose. It smells like sticky sweat on skin, like worn-out cologne expired over the day, like pasty musk deodorant mixed with green-apple shampoo. A smell I want to bottle so I can open it up at will and wash it all over me.

"So why do you think your grades have slipped?" he asks.

"I don't know," I say. "I guess I just have other stuff on my mind."

"Oh yeah?" He closes his book. "Like what?"

I flip the pages forward and back in my textbook, my eyes scanning down the review questions in chapter ten, even though the test is on chapter seven.

"If there's something bothering you, you can tell me," he says. "Did you get another prank after we hung up?"

"No."

"Relax, then. He's not calling now, is he? Maybe he knows I'm here."

"Why do you say that?" I ask.

"I don't know. Maybe he only wants to call when you're alone. Or at least when it's just girls around. Maybe a guy would intimidate him."

I feel myself swallow. Chad's eyes travel over my neck to notice the gesture.

"I wish he *would* call while I was here," he says.

"Why?" I ask.

"Because at least you'd know for sure it wasn't me."

Yikes! A huge allegation, but I can't object. "Is that how you think I feel?"

He shifts from Drea's bed to mine, plunking down atop a bunch of papers, making me scoot over to avoid hip touchage. "I don't know. How *do* you feel?"

I focus down on my notebook, on the three-dimensional trapezoid scribbled near the spiral. I can't look at him. I can't answer what he's asking me—the same question that's been looming over our heads for the three years we've known each other.

I flip a page in my notebook to stall. "How do I feel about what?"

I feel him get all frustrated. He swivels his baseball cap around so that the visor sticks out in back. "About me?" he says. "How do you feel about me?"

I can't believe he's actually saying it. Actually asking it in real, live, verbal language. I look around the room for something, some idea to segue myself out of this line of questioning. There, sticking out from beneath his left butt-cheek, is one of my lab reports.

"You're sitting on my nanoclusters," I say.

"Huh?"

Did I really just say that? I motion with a nod at the report beneath his perfectly rounded butt cheeks, and he slides the thing out, all mangled from sittage. Still, the newly formed butt-indentations in the soft white paper almost make me want to frame it.

"Just tell me," he says—his face completely serious. "I need to know."

"You want to know if I think you're the one who's been stalking Drea?" I feel so dumb talking this way, asking questions that purposely skirt the real question, but I just can't bring myself to admit it. Not until I know for sure it's over between him and Drea.

"Okay," he says. "To start with. *Do* you?"

I look into his eyes and really consider the question and how I feel. I think about the dream I had of him at the window. How his jersey disappeared from our room, but then he was the one to show up wearing it, claiming that someone left it in his mailbox along with one of the notes.

I think about how he tried to scare us with the hockey mask, how he's always calling at just the right time, and how we saw him on the pay phone in front of the library just minutes after one of the pranks.

I think how it kind of makes sense, how it would be the perfect way to get Drea off his back. Or just punish her for playing so many mind games over the years.

And then I think how disappointed I'd be if it really was him.

I study his face for some flinch or falter, anything that might give me some sign that it isn't him, that he isn't involved. But I just can't tell. I just don't know.

"Well?" he asks.

"Are you the one?"

"I wish you didn't have to ask."

"Is that a no?"

He shakes his head and lifts my chin with a finger, the minty smell of his toothpaste filling the air between us. He moves in toward me, stopping just inches from my mouth, so close that I can see the tiny points of baby-blond that surround his upper lip.

"Wait, is that a yes? I have to know, Chad."

I hate myself for asking, for being so loyal, for having to know the truth, for caring either way. He moves even closer, so near that the skin of our lips touches. Soft and moist and hot-tea minty. It makes me want to burst out crying out of mere frustration. But I don't. I keep my eyes from fluttering closed, my lips from quivering against his. And wait for the answer.

"It's a yes," he says, finally. "I am the one." He closes his eyes and presses his lips fully against mine. At first I don't know if I should kiss him back, but then my mouth just does. A full-lip, tongue-twirling, tingle-all-over kiss.

When we break, my eyes remain on his mouth, almost afraid that if I look up into his eyes, I'll wake out of the most blissful sleep. He touches my cheek with the nubs of his fingers and then brings my lips up for one more taste.

"I've been waiting to do that since the last time," he says.

"Really?" I try to stop the smile on my face.

"Remember?" His eyes shift from my mouth to my eyes. "The last time?"

I nod.

He moves in for another kiss, but my words pause him. "When you said that you were the one, you didn't mean you were *the* one, I mean the one who's after Drea, did you?"

"What do *you* think?"

"I don't think you are." And I *don't* think he is. But I still want—need—to hear him say it.

He smiles at me, relieved, and leans in for that kiss.

"What about Drea?" I say, stopping him again. "I mean, what about how she feels about you?"

"She doesn't really feel anything about me." He sighs and draws his mouth away from mine. "She just *thinks* she does. If I wanted to ask her out again—and I don't, but if I did—she'd say yes, enjoy the victory for a few days, and then want to break up. It's always been like that with her, like some game."

"Do you think that maybe you still have feelings for her?"

"Sure, I mean, we've grown up together. I care about her. A lot. Just not the way she thinks she wants." He takes my hands and sandwiches them between his own, sending warm and sparkly tingles up and down my back. "Me and Drea get along much better as friends."

"Is that why you want someone else?"

"Don't you get it? I don't care about someone else."

Our eyes lock and I'm not sure what comes over me, if it's the way his eyebrows furrow, begging me to understand him, the way his lips sit, begging to be kissed, or pure, unadulterated, all-American hormones, but all of a sudden, I'm on him. My hands, my mouth, my lips, my heart. We kiss—a long, soft, pulpy, winter-under-the-blankets-by-the-fire kiss. But then I push him away. "We can't," I say, all out of breath. "We can't do this. I mean, I want to, but . . . ."

Chad wraps his arms around my shoulders and holds me to his chest. I listen to the rhythm of his heart beating and give up on saying anything more. I only want to cry.

twenty

There is no way any studying is going to get done now. I'm sitting on my bed, flipping pages back and forth between chapter summaries, running my eyes over the columns of meaningless physics terms, but my mind is not absorbing anything at all.

"Maybe we should get some fresh air," Chad suggests, closing his book.

I nod, relieved to change the scenery, hoping the cool night air will shake me out of this funk.

And as if by some celestial force, we end up at the tree where we first kissed, though neither of us points it out. Instead, we just walk by it, flashlights in hand, beyond the lawn and into the woods, making awkward small talk about hockey schedules and Chinese food, about things that don't even seem to matter right now.

The woods smell sort of musky tonight, like salty skin and perfume mixed, like hot and sticky summer nights in a tent. I breathe the scent in, hoping it will linger on my clothes and in my hair so I can savor it later on.

"I'll be right back," Chad says. "Nature calls."

I nod and look away while he disappears behind a clump of trees. I wait for several minutes before getting concerned. "Chad?" I call. "Is everything okay?" When he doesn't answer I make my way toward the cluster of trees where he headed. I find myself lifting branches and swiping brush from in front of my eyes, walking farther and farther, expecting to find him.

But I don't.

Instead, I arrive at a clearing. I peer between two long and leafy branches sticking out in my path and see a large, wooden structure of some sort, highlighted by the moon.

"Chad!" I shout. "Come out, now!"

The structure is almost houselike—naked wooden planks like right out of a lumberyard, boards nailed together to form a giant, square base, and individual planks sticking up straight like walls.

Did Chad bring me here on purpose? Does he think this is funny?

"Chad!" I shout toward the structure. "You're scaring me."

I go to take another step, but then stop. Listen. Someone's following me. I can hear them. Can hear their footsteps crunching down against the fallen leaves and twigs.

Pain bubbles up in my stomach. I have to pee. Now! Out
of the corner of my eye I spot one of those portable bathrooms, the mint-green kind you see at amusement parks. I
squish my inner thighs together and walk as best I can toward it, using the light of the moon to guide my way. But
before I know it, my foot has stepped into a ditch, and I'm
on my way down, my left cheek smacking hard against the
powdery dirt.

A light shines on from somewhere inside the house in response. I lift myself out of the ditch and sit back on my
heels. There are letters dug into the ground. Long, straight
letters, at least a foot long. They spell out DREA.

I step around her name and head for the porta-john, still
several yards away. I need to know if anyone is in that
house. If they are the ones who turned on the light or dug
Drea's name in the dirt. If Chad is the one following at my
heels, trying to scare me out of my wits. But first, I have to
pee; there's no contest.

My stomach aches with each step. But I make it, and
turn the handle on the door. Locked. "Chad? Are you in
there?" I smash my thighs together; hear myself whimper
like a pup. I wait a few moments. Nothing. Silence. A dark,
lonely, nighttime silence.

Someone is inside.

I back up, feel my chest heave in and out, my breath almost independent of me. Chad would answer me. He
wouldn't joke for this long. He knows how scared I got
about the phone calls.

I glance toward the doorlike opening of the house and run inside. A spotlight meets me with a clunk against my forehead. It hangs from a support beam, just below the partial roof, and lights up the whole area. I rub the spot and look around. Boards have been erected to create one long hallway with adjoining rooms to the left and right.

A ripping sound, like heavy tape, is coming from somewhere down the hallway. "Chad?" I call. "Is that you?"

The noise stops.

"This isn't funny, you know." I half-expect to find him in one of the rooms with some clichéd idea of romance—like a candlelit picnic or a room full of daisies—even though we've mutually decided to keep things platonic. I jam my hand between my legs and slowly begin down the hallway, the rubber soles of my yellow sneakers squeaking slightly against the wooden floor.

There are four doors to choose from, two on each side. I decide to head toward the one closest to me on the right. It has the largest archway, and from this angle, I can already see through to an empty corner. I take two steps forward, then stop, hearing a board creak somewhere in front of me.

"Stacey?" a voice whispers.

And then the light goes out.

I hobble back in the direction of the main door-frame, my fingers practically pinching closed the folds of skin between my legs. With my other hand, I pat along the walls, making my way back down the hallway, plank by plank, so I can guide my way out. But it's like the hallway doesn't end, just keeps going on and on.

What is wrong? Why am I not out yet? Why haven't I even made it back into the front room?

Twenty-six planks of wood later, I stop looking for the entryway. Instead, desperate, I assess the gaps between the wooden planks. About six inches wide. I poke my arm all the way through a gap and feel the wind fly through my fingers. Freedom is on the other side, I'm sure of it. And if I can squeeze my body through, I will be back outside, in the forest, and can make my way back to campus.

Footsteps make their way down the hallway toward me. I take a deep breath, suck my belly in, and push, shoulder-first, into the gap. I angle my head sideways to fit; jut my pelvis forward; kick my leg through. But it's no use. The planks of wood pinch into my ribs where my bones and flesh won't budge. There's no doubting it now—I'm trapped inside.

A phone rings from one of the rooms.

"It's for you, Stacey," says a voice.

The voice. *Him.* And it's so close to me, like just beyond my fingertips.

"Better get it," he says.

Nine rings, ten.

"Get the phone, Stacey!" he yells, as though through clenched teeth.

I walk toward the scream of the phone, the sting below my abdomen reminding me I have to pee.

"Getting warmer."

The sound of the ringing grows louder with each step. My arm outstretched, I walk in search of the phone, my other hand still squelching the pee back. I step through an opening and a light comes on. A spotlight—hanging down from one of the roof planks. It illuminates a pay phone on the wall directly in front of me. And still ringing.

"It's for you, Stacey," the voice repeats.

I pick up the receiver and feel my lower half release—my pants fill up with warm and wet. "Hello?" I whisper, trying to make it sound as though I'm not crying, not feeling sorry for myself, not scared half to death.

"Hello to you, Stacey," he says. "Time's almost up. Only two more lilies left in our bouquet."

"Who is this?"

"Love is funny, Stacey. Didn't you know that?" I can feel his breath on the back of my neck. He's right behind me.

I swirl around and meet his eyes with mine. "I can't believe it," I whisper. "It's you."

twenty-one

I sit up with a gasp.

"Stace?"

I blink my eyes and look around. I'm still in my room. Still in my white tank top and Drea's pajama bottoms.

And Chad is still beside me, in my bed.

I shift slightly, to check if I really wet myself.

I did.

The clock reads 6:15 A.M. We slept for over four hours.

"Did you have a bad dream?" He sits up and wipes at his eyes.

I know I saw the stalker's face in my dream. But now, sitting up in bed, the rush of reality all around me, I just can't remember it.

"You should go," I say.

But he doesn't move.

"Please." I shake Chad's hand from my shoulder.

"Hey," he says. "Why are you acting so scared of me?"

"I'm not. Just go. *Go!*"

"Is this about what happened last night? Because—"

"Nothing happened last night," I snap.

"Not nothing," he says.

It's quiet between us for several seconds. I clench my teeth and feel an ache in my jaw.

"How about everything we talked about?" he asks. "You know, if things were different—"

"Well, they aren't," I say.

"I guess that's just it," he says. "I'll wait until they are, if that's cool with you. Because last night wasn't just nothing for me."

I hate him for being so perfect. I hate that he cares and that I care back. I hate sitting here, having to beg him to leave so I can clean up the mess.

"You don't have to say anything," he continues. "I just wanted you to know that."

I gather the covers around my legs, feeling the warmth in my pants, feeling the tears storm down my cheeks.

"Are you cold?" He removes the covers from his middle and places them over me.

I nod, squishing the comforter over my lap. "Please go, Chad."

"I don't want to leave with you upset."

"*Go!*" I plead. "Leave me alone."

"Why? Why are you doing this?"

"Because I don't care about you," I spout. A deadly stinger.

Chad sinks back in his chest from the blow. "I don't believe you," he says, after a pause. His voice is all scratchy, like I've made him bleed from the inside out.

He stands up from the bed and looks away to hide his face. His body looks tired, defeated, like I could crumple it up into a paper ball and toss it away.

He bends down to put on his shoes and that's when Drea comes in.

Drea!

I watch the smile on her face melt. She studies the picture of Chad and me: Chad, reaching for a sneaker, his clothes from yesterday hanging in a giant wrinkle on his body, and me, still lying in bed. She looks from his bed-head hair to the pant leg, stuck up around one knee.

"Drea—" he says.

She turns to me, a cupful of coffee and a wax paper bag slipping from her grip, landing splat against the floor. "I brought you breakfast."

I open my mouth to say something, but all the words that come to mind—this isn't what it looks like, it was an accident, we fell asleep—sound completely pathetic.

"Drea, before you freak out—" Chad takes a step toward her, exposing the side of his face with the bed-ruffle imprint.

"Don't speak to me!" she says.

"Drea—" I begin.

"How could you do this to me?" she shouts.

"Nothing happened," I say.

"She's right," Chad says. "Nothing happened. I came over to study and we fell asleep."

"No wonder why you didn't answer my calls last night."

"What?"

"Don't act all innocent with me. I tried to call you last night, like I said I would, but you wouldn't answer. Too busy, I guess."

I look toward the night table, but the phone isn't there. I glance around and spot the cord sticking out from beneath a pile of dirty clothes. "Drea, I didn't hear it ring."

"Fuck you!" she says, her eyes welling up with tears.

"Drea, we were studying and fell asleep."

"Right. Amber warned me about this, about how much you like him."

Ouch! Did Amber really tell her that?

"Come on, Dray," Chad says, "let's not make this bigger than it is. I called here because I have this massive physics test tomorrow—I mean, today—"

"I guess you didn't have a problem hearing *his* call," she says.

"Anyway," Chad continues, "I thought that maybe you guys would be pulling an all-nighter. But then Stacey told me that that freak was pranking her and she couldn't sleep. So I told her I'd come over and we could study."

"How thoughtful of you," she says.

"What's wrong with that?" Chad says.

"Fuck you, too."

"How about this, Drea," he says, "when you're finished with your tantrum, give me a call." He grabs his cap off the night table and tugs it over his bed-head.

"Don't hold your breath."

"Look," he says, "Stacey is a friend of mine and if that bothers you—"

"*What?!*"

"It's not like we're still going out," he says. "We're all just friends."

"You're no friend," she says. "Neither of you." She turns her back on us to fish into her mini-fridge. She takes out a half-eaten bar of chocolate and tears down the wrapper.

There's a knock on the door. "Girls?"

Madame Discharge.

"There's a lot of noise coming from your room," she says. "Is everything okay?"

"Fine," Drea says.

"Is Stacey okay?"

Chad looks around for someplace to hide, but it's useless; the closets are stuffed to maximum capacity, and there's no way he's getting under my bed.

"I should let you fry," Drea whispers to him.

"I'm fine, Ms. LaCharge," I call. "I'm just getting dressed."

"Well, I need to come in for a sec," she says.

Chad looks at me one last time before booting it out the window. Two seconds later, Drea opens the door. Madame Discharge looks around the room—her tiny gray eyes swallowed up by a pair of clunky, red glasses. "What's all the noise?"

"We were just arguing about whether or not I should cut my hair," Drea says.

"Oh?" Madame Discharge visually assesses Drea's locks. "Yeah, a little pixie might be cute on you." She scratches at the thought, her finger rubbing over at least five chin hairs.

"We really need to get dressed." I add a pillow to the pig-pile of bedding on my lap and a wave of Chad's cologne swims across my face.

"Okay," Madame says. "Just keep it down. We've had a few complaints about you two."

"We will, Ms. LaCharge. Thank you." Drea closes the door behind her.

"Drea—" I begin.

"Don't!"

"You can't just not talk to me," I say.

"Why can't I?"

"Because we're friends."

"Friends don't shit on one another."

"You don't believe me that nothing happened?"

"Oh, I believe it." She stands at the foot of my bed with her arms folded. "But not because you didn't *want* something to happen."

"What are you saying?" I press my thighs together, feeling the dampness of *her* pajamas stick against my skin.

"I'm saying that you lied to Chad about getting prank calls last night, so he'd feel sorry for you and come over here."

"That's not what happened."

"Then what *did* happen?" She flips up the end of the covers, exposing my bare feet.

"Nothing. We already told you that." I kick the covers back down as best I can, feeling now, more than ever, imprisoned in this bed until everyone leaves.

"Did you kiss him?"

"Drea—"

"Did you?"

I know it's weak, that it will come back to me threefold, but right now, I'll take it. I just want to be left alone. "No," I say, finally.

"Liar." She tosses her candy bar down on the bed. "What else did you do with him?" She grabs the end of the comforter and peeks underneath.

"No, Drea! Please, don't!"

Drea raises an eyebrow at my response. "What am I not supposed to see?" She yanks the comforter from my legs and the pillows go flying.

"Aren't those *my* pajamas?"

Tears slide down the sides of my face as I wait for her to notice. And when she does, it's even more humiliating than I ever imagined.

"You wet the bed?"

"Drea—" I cry, trying to cover my lap with my hands. "Please . . . don't tell anyone."

"Oh my god!" She looks like she doesn't know whether to gag or guffaw. *"You wet the bed!"*

I bury my face into the pillow, ostrich-style, as though she won't be able to see me, as though I will just disappear.

twenty-two

Why did I decide to come to school today? How in the world am I supposed to take a physics test after everything that happened last night?

Question number one already has way too many variables. How am I supposed to know what the W of a brick equals under G conditions when I didn't even know bricks had Ws or experienced Gs in the first place? I look up from my scrabble of letters at Chad, seated three seats in front of me to the right. I wonder if he knows about the bedwetting, if Drea's already told him.

I try to blink him out of my mind and instead concentrate on last night's nightmare. On the stalker's face. I know I recognized who it was, but now, fully awake, my memory of the face is just gone. I need to go back to the dorm and try to get it back somehow.

The bell rings and that's my cue. I scribble my name across the top so the teacher knows who to give the big fat zero to, hand it in first, and dart out the door. But, unfortunately, I'm not quick enough. Chad stops me about two doors down the hallway.

"I'm sorry about last night," he says, mussing a hand through his hair. "I mean, what happened between you and Drea."

"It's no big deal."

"Yeah it is and you know it."

I look away, wondering what he'd think of me if he knew my secret, if he'd still feel the same way.

"Has Drea said anything to you?" I ask. "I mean, is she talking to you?" I focus a moment on his lips, remembering their every detail from the night before—the tiny yellow freckle over the vee at the top, the threadlike scar in the left corner at the bottom. Proof that last night really happened. That I really kissed him.

"Yeah, she's talking to me," he says. "She was mad at first in English. You know, played all pouty and standoffish. But then she got over it. I tried to talk to her about not being so mad at you, but she didn't listen. I don't get why she's mad at you and not me."

"Because you're the guy," I say.

A conversation stopper.

"Anyway," he says, "I'm kind of glad last night happened, I mean, aside from getting you two in a fight."

"You are?"

"Yeah, I mean, she can't keep thinking of me like her property. Like I said last night, Drea and I make better friends. It's the only time we actually get along."

"Glad I was there to help." I throw my backpack over my shoulder and turn to walk away.

"Wait." Chad touches my arm to stop me.

"What?" I pull my arm away.

"That's not what I meant."

"Then what did you mean?"

"I meant just what I said—I'm glad it happened."

"Does Drea know how you feel? Have you actually told her everything you've told me, about the two of you being just friends?"

He thinks about it a second. "Well, I haven't actually put it into words, but I'm sure she knows."

"Maybe she doesn't know as much as you think she does. Or maybe you don't know what you want."

"I know what I want," he says.

I look up at him and now *he's* the one looking at *my* mouth, *my* lips. And I want more than anything to bite them, to lick them, to suck them up into my face or cover them with my hand. But instead I smile and he smiles back. And suddenly I feel trapped in some goofy toothpaste commercial, the kind where the actors get all lovey on each other from the sheer glow of each other's teeth.

We linger there for a bit, not quite knowing what to say or how to leave things. In the twenty or so awkward seconds, as we shuffle our feet—mine, a pair of Doc Marten knockoffs, his, shiny black Sketchers with silver buckles—I try to honestly ask myself whether or not I'd erase last night, including Drea finding out about my secret, if I could.

But the answer is a big, fat, walloping *no*.

"I gotta go," he says. "I guess I'll see you around."

"I guess so," I say, not knowing if I should jump into his arms or high-five him, midair.

We do neither. Chad stuffs his hands into his pockets and walks off toward his next class. I, on the other hand, feign migraine sickness and get excused from B-Block English. There's really no sense in screwing up any more grades today. Plus, I have way more pressing matters to tend to than a discussion of *The Canterbury Tales*. I have a stalker's face to conjure up, for god's sake. Hopefully a memory spell will help.

. . .

Back in the room, I plop myself down on the bed and take a few seconds to reflect on what I do remember. I know that my nightmares took me into the forest again, and that this time there was some sort of structure waiting for me. I remember the planks of wood, the open doorways, and Drea's name carved in the dirt. I remember the spotlight, hearing the phone ring, and even answering it. But when I try to picture the person standing behind me, whispering in my ear, everything goes fuzzy.

I grab the family scrapbook and run a finger down the partial list of contents at the beginning. There are several spells for memory, but only one that specifies it can help reveal the person you dreamed about. It was written by my great-great aunt Delia. I turn the fragile pages until I reach the spell, and notice right away that a couple of the ingredients are covered with droplets of wax. I try to scrape the clumps away, but it doesn't work. I'll have to piece things together as best I can.

I remove the few beauty items I own—a nude lipstick, a mauve eye shadow, and a tube of body glitter (a stocking stuffer from my mother two Christmases ago)—from the circular mirror on my dresser. I place the mirror flat on the floor and unscrew the lid off a jar of black poster paint.

The reflection of myself as I look down into the mirror reminds me of Gram. I move my hair away from my face in a hand-held ponytail and notice for the first time that I have her golden-brown eyes—not just the color, but the way they sit deep in the sockets, sort of bedroom-sexy, like Bette Davis—and how the lashes curl up at the ends.

I light a thick blue candle and place it on a silver dish. Gram used to light one just like it, every night before bed, but it wasn't until I was twelve that I inquired about the color. I remember her looking up at me, her eyes heavy, like tiny hammocks sagged in the skin pockets underneath. She extinguished the candle with a snuffer and frowned at my question. Still, she answered it—an answer that to this day makes me wonder: "Because blue is for nightmares," she said. "To make them go away or bring them closer, depending on how you use it."

"You get nightmares?"

She nodded.

"Every night?"

She pushed the dish of sugar cookies toward me. "Eat the last couple," she said. "They'll just go to waste."

I nodded and took one. I chewed it slowly, wondering if she could hear the crunching in my mouth, waiting for her to tell me more—to tell me for what purpose she used the blue candle—but she didn't. She looked tired and deflated, as though those eye-hammocks might collapse at any moment. I watched her curl up on the sofa—her body like a flannel-covered *g*—and waited until she slept. I wondered if the blue candle really helped, or if there were nightmares alive in her mind at that moment.

Unfortunately, I never asked.

.   .   .

The flame flickers three times after I light it. And I feel a chill pass over my shoulders, almost as if the temperature in the room has suddenly dropped. But instead of freaking me out, the feeling comforts me. Because I know in my heart that Gram is here, watching over me, guiding me just like old times.

I dip a paintbrush into the jar and begin making sideways strokes, west to east, across the mirror's surface, until the glass is completely covered in black. "The spirit of dreams is everlasting," I whisper. "It lives within my mind."

I fill a mug with water from the sink and place it in Drea's mini-microwave. The directions say I'm supposed to drink a full cup of chamomile tea, rotating the cup counter-clockwise with each sip.

When the water's ready, I dangle the tea bag inside, al-lowing the curls of steam to drift up into my face and fill me with the chamomile flower's ability to soothe.

I crack open four cardamom seeds and group their tiny, brown, pelletlike contents into my palm. "The spirit of dreams is everlasting," I say, sprinkling them into the tea. "It lives within my soul."

I reflect a moment on the missing ingredients, and de-cide to use a teaspoon of mashed banana for prophecy and a sprinkling of thyme for strength and courage. I add these to the mug and stir counterclockwise with a freshly washed spoon. "The spirit of dreams is everlasting. It lives within my heart."

I take a sip, concentrating on the flavors inside and their ability to help grant me the vision I need. "May the spirit within my dreams show itself in my mind, my soul, and my heart." I rotate the mug with each sip until there's nothing left, then place the mirror in my lap and stare down into it. "Vision of darkness. Vision of light. Vision in daytime. Vi-sion in night. To the north, south, east, and west, may my vision of you come out of rest."

The spell says the face of the person I dreamed about will begin to appear out of the blackness. I stare hard at the mirror for several minutes, trying to make shapes and fea-tures where there's just plain nothing. I look over every inch, wondering if maybe I should try wiping at the black-ness to see the face underneath.

With a finger, I clear away a tiny circle of the wet paint in the center. I look down. Still nothing. Using my palms, I start wiping away the black, my hands and arms getting completely covered in paint as I struggle to make the glass clear again.

I look down into the mirror one last time, but the only face that appears is my own. And the only one I can't seem to get out of my stupid, *stupid* head is Chad's.

The whole idea of it—of not getting the spell to work, of preoccupying myself with thoughts of Chad at a time like this—makes me want to toss the mirror right out the window, breaking the glass all over again. Instead, in one last pathetic attempt at trying to see something, I pick up the tea mug and study the glob inside—the mixture of banana and spices sitting at the bottom with the tea bag—now soiled with my negative energy and impatience. Still, I wait several moments, as if the mixture will change in some way and reveal information, but it only seems to get muddier.

I fish a towel from the dirty pile on the floor and wipe the paint from my hands and arms. I look at the directions again, trying to make out the words hidden beneath the clumps of wax. But it's no use. It will take me years to experiment with different ingredients and get the spell right, and maybe even longer than that to actually make it work.

I dump the contents of the mug into the trash, spring back onto my bed, and curl up into a ball inside my covers. Tears roll down my cheeks, sliding onto the pillow. I don't understand it. I thought Gram was with me; I thought she was going to help me. And now I feel more alone than ever.

I wipe my eyes and look at my amethyst ring. As much as I hate to admit it, I know exactly what Gram would say right now, what she always used to say about spells when they didn't work—how it isn't the spell that fails the witch, it's the witch that fails the spell.

When things like this happened to her, she would try and go back to the root of the spell, the reason she was conducting it in the first place. She would try to figure out what she could on her own, reminding herself, reminding me, that spells aid us in what we want to do or know; they don't do the work for us.

I drag the covers up over my chin, wondering if I already have all I need to figure this whole thing out. If maybe I'm just not thinking hard enough. Or maybe I'm thinking too much. I glance over at the clock. It's a little after four—just an hour before dinner time. I'm anything but hungry, but I know I have to face them all—to see if Drea said anything, to tell Veronica that we should work on a plan tonight.

And to see Chad again.

twenty-three

Dinner time. I spot Veronica by the condiment table, busy picking the egg slices out of her salad. I wave, but she ignores me—like last night in the café, when she made the great transformation from Veronica the Villain to Veronica the Victim, never even existed.

I take a plate piled high with the dinner *du jour*—turkey fricassee: perfect cubes of mystery meat smothered in a gray and chunky cream sauce over a sticky ball of rice. Indi-gestible. I trade it for a wrapped tuna sandwich and walk over to the condiment table. Veronica's still there, still working on ridding all the evil yolk bits from the lettuce leaves. She notices me and takes a step away, like it's grade school all over again and I have cooties.

"Why don't you come sit with us?" I say. "You know, so we can talk about tomorrow."

"I don't think so," she says, waving her red acrylic nails in my face.

"Why? We agreed yesterday that we'd come up with a plan. Tomorrow's the day."

"Oh, that. I guess I was tweaked out at first. But after talking it out with my real friends, I know exactly who the stalker is."

"You do?"

"Think about it. This isn't a slasher movie, it's a prep school. Obviously someone who doesn't like me—" She pauses as Drea walks by. "Someone who's probably jealous of me, who can't hold onto her man, is trying pretty hard to scare me. Not gonna work."

"Don't you think—"

"What I think is that it seems pretty obvious who that person is, seeing that she's been supposedly getting stalked too."

"You think Drea made this up?"

"What else am I supposed to think? She hates me. Hates that I talk to Chad. Is jealous whenever I go near him."

"Wait," I say. "This has absolutely nothing to do with Drea being jealous over Chad."

"Are you kidding?" She takes a step closer to me. "This has *everything* to do with her being jealous. Just you wait. One day, very soon, Chad and I will be together. What will Drea do then?"

"Just stop, Veronica; you're talking crazy. I know it's not Drea. I know she's not making this up."

"You're her best friend. Why should I believe you?"

"Because I know. Look, whether you like it or not, we're going to help you."

"Save it for the movies, Stacey. A little too drama-fest for me." She pulls a handful of napkins from the dispenser and pokes a straw into her iced tea. "Oh, and when Drea's ready to 'come and get me,' tell her I'll be on the jock side." She motions to the right side of the cafeteria and then makes her way in that direction.

I look toward the left side, where I normally sit. Drea, Amber, and PJ are already engrossed in conversation. I'll just have to get Drea and Amber's help to convince Veronica that we need to collaborate. Even though I'm not completely sold on all the details of Veronica's story, I'm not willing to just cast it off as fiction. I definitely think it's possible that she too could be in danger. I also think that helping her out might help us help Drea.

I collect a two-inch stack of napkins, extra straws if anyone needs one, and a wide assortment of condiments, ranging from mustard to jam. At least six people come to the condiment table while I'm stalling here, arranging everything in neat little rows on my tray. I wonder what the three of them are talking about and if I'll be welcome.

But more importantly, I wonder what Drea told them about this morning.

I make my way to the table, my hands keeping steady by gripping firmly onto the tray. "Hi guys," I say.

"Hey, Stace," PJ says. "What's up?"

"Not much." I park it beside Amber and peek up at Drea, who is already looking away.

"Have an extra straw, why don't you," Amber says.

"Thought you guys might need an extra," I say.

"I could." PJ grabs a handful of them and begins blowing the wrappers at us.

"Bug off, PJ!" Amber says, pulling a wrapper from her hair.

"So what are we all talking about?" I ask.

Amber looks up at Drea and I catch an exchange of snickers. "Nothing much. Just bitching about how little time we have between classes. You know, like, how hard it is to make it from building to building in such short time." Amber picks at the turkey fricassee with her chopsticks. "And how they're building a new admissions house on, like, the other side of the woods."

"Stopped building, you mean," Drea says.

"Oh yeah, because our school's so poor, they can't even finish what they start."

"You have to wonder where all the money goes," I say, relaxing enough to peel down the spout of my milk carton and actually take a sip.

"You know," Amber begins, "the other day I had to go all the way from O'Brian to Remington Building because Mr. Farcus' class didn't have heat and we had to change rooms."

"Were you late?" PJ smooshes a handful of corn chips inside his tuna sandwich.

"How could I not have been? That's, like, five miles."

"Well, it wasn't your fault," I say. "Teachers have to understand how hard it is, especially in the snow. I don't know how they expect us to do it in under four minutes."

"And what do you do when you have to go to the bathroom?" Amber says. "What? Am I supposed to pee in my pants right there in the middle of class?"

While Amber and Drea exchange giggles, I try to decide whether plastic drinking straws make suitable eye-gouging material.

"You know what they need?" Amber says. "One of those portable bathrooms, you know, like they have at the carnival?" Amber and Drea laugh out loud.

"What's so funny?" PJ asks.

"Private joke," Drea says.

"Very private," Amber says, elbowing me.

"Don't you think it's about time we start sharing privates, Amb?" PJ asks.

"Try never," Amber says. She turns, wraps her arms around my shoulders, and kisses me full on the cheek with glittery, sea-green lips. "Love ya," she says.

"Hey, how 'bout a little over here." PJ puckers up, a blob of tuna hanging from his bottom lip.

"Kiss this," Amber says, slapping her fanny.

"With pleasure," he says, taking a huge bite out of his sandwich.

"I think I've just lost my appetite." Amber throws her chopsticks down.

"Me too," I say.

Amber and I look at each other and I can't help but laugh—first a nervous giggle, then a full-fledged, belly-jiggling guffaw right along with her. Drea clears her throat and swivels toward the aisle, away from the table.

"Drea," I say. "We really need to talk."

"What-ev-er," she says.

"No, we do. I know you're mad at me, but we need to put that aside for now and come up with a plan to help Veronica."

"Come on, Dray," Amber says, blowing a straw wrapper at her ear. "Loosen up and play Buffy with us tonight. I feel like slaying demons."

"Drea," I say, "I told you nothing happened last night."

"I know nothing happened," Drea says. "You're not exactly his type."

"What's that supposed to mean?"

"We used to date, remember?"

"Whoa, that's news to me," PJ says. "You guys used to date?" He points back and forth between me and Drea.

"No, stupid," Amber says, flicking a turkey cube at him, "Chad and Drea."

"Oh."

Drea swivels back toward the table. "Why would he go for you when he has me?"

"Drea, let's not go there," I say. "You're obviously still really upset." I look at Amber to help me out, but she's decided to stay as neutral as Swiss cheese, busying herself by trying to get her chopsticks to stand up straight in the gooey mound of turkey fricassee.

"Think about it," Drea says. "He dates me on and off for three years and then decides to completely change his taste and go for you? Doesn't happen."

"I don't know," I say. "Maybe he just thinks you're a bitch."

"Meow," PJ says.

More like a full-blown roar. I hate talking to her this way. I hate having some guy come between us. It isn't worth it.

"Why don't we ask him?" Drea says. "Hey, Chad!" She straightens herself up on the seat and waves him over.

"I'm glad to see you guys talking again," he says, standing right behind me now.

"Would somebody please tell me what is going on?" PJ massages his temples.

"Chad," Drea begins, "Stacey wants to know if you think I'm a bitch. Do you?"

I can feel my cheeks crimson over, a burning combination of anger and grief.

Chad looks at me, his eyebrows arching up. "Is that what you told her?"

"No."

"I'm going back to the room." Drea stands up from the table.

"No, Drea," I say. "Not alone. Plus, we still need to talk. We need to decide about tomorrow. It's as much for Veronica as it is for you."

Drea stands there a moment, perhaps mulling the idea over, her pride struggling with her common sense. I know she wants to help us plan. But I also know she's more hurt and angry than I've ever seen her.

"Veronica?" Chad asks.

"Group project," Amber clarifies.

Chad still looks confused, but he doesn't question it. "Come on, Dray." He pats my shoulder for support and I watch Drea's eyes zoom in on the gesture.

"'Come on' *what*? As far as I'm concerned, Chad, you can have her. But I'm warning you, you'd better be careful. She wets the bed."

My heart falls to the floor and shatters into a million pieces. Is this really happening?

"*Drea!*" Amber shouts.

"What? It was funny only a few minutes ago." Drea looks at Chad. "Just ask her."

PJ lets out a gasp, launching a straw wrapper into the air.

"This is ridiculous," Chad says. "Drea, I don't know what you're talking about, but just stop. Listen to yourself."

"Just ask her. What I'd like to know is whether she wet the bed before or after you left this morning."

The table goes quiet for seconds, practically test-taking conditions, the question just looming around my head.

"What are you talking about?" Chad says finally. He looks at Drea and then at me. "What is she talking about?"

But I can't even look at him. I can only stare down into my tray, waiting for the moment to pass, as if that's possible.

"Total ass," Amber says to Drea, in my defense. "I can't *believe* you just said that."

I can't believe it either. The whole idea of it time-travels me back to grammar school, with its playground bullies, all over again. My jaw aches from the severe grind of my teeth. I can't bear to sit here any longer. I get up from the table and walk away, grateful that no one decides to follow me.

twenty-four

It takes Chad two whole hours to find me in the library, and when he does, I'm hidden away in one of the study carrels in the very back, mentally decaying from breathing in all the musty fumes of old and decrepit books.

"I guess I beat Amber." He pulls a chair from the carrel behind me and sits down.

"Amber?"

"She's looking for you, too."

"Oh," I say, not looking up.

"We've been looking everywhere," he says. "What are you doing?"

"Studying." I flash him the cover of my French book—a group of teens eating baguette sandwiches in a park—but keep focused on the yellow grammar box in the middle of the page, my focal point. "Madame LeSnore's gonna let me retake that test I fell asleep in."

"Do you want me to quiz you?"

"Not really."

"Can you at least look at me?"

I roll my eyes and manage to look toward the side of his face. "Okay?"

"I'm just trying to be a friend here," he says.

"Yeah, well, I've had enough friends for one day."

"Do you mean that?" he asks.

No. But, of course, I don't say that. I busy my fingers by folding over the corners of my book pages, hoping my silence tells him for me.

"Look," he says. "I don't know what's going on exactly, but if you want to talk about it, I'll listen."

I doubt I'll ever want to discuss my bedwetting with Chad, but I appreciate the offer. "You must think I'm some kind of freak," I say.

"Actually, I think you're pretty great." He places his hand on my forearm and smiles at me, like nothing's changed. So maybe nothing has. The moment is filled with awkward sweetness, like one of us should say something to break things up. That's where Amber steps in.

"Kodak moment," she sings. She takes a picture of us with her invisible camera.

"Where did you come from?" I say, moving my arm from Chad's touch.

"Are you kidding? I've been everywhere." She wipes an invisible stream of sweat from her forehead. "Never thought to look in the library. Have you been in here all this time? I'm surprised your skin isn't sallow. See what studying does to you? Shuts you off from civilization." She points toward my evil books.

"A little civilization severance is fine with me tonight."

"No deal," she says. "We have major business to attend to."

"I think I can take a hint," Chad says. He turns to me. "I'll talk to you later."

I nod, half-wanting him to stay, but knowing he can't. Drea, Amber, and I need to make a plan for tomorrow.

"See ya," Amber says, hula-dancing a goodbye to him. And just as soon as he rounds the corner, she grabs my arm. "Dish."

"What?" I say, smiling. "Nothing."

"You two were way too cozy for nothing. Dish."

"I should really be mad at you," I say.

"Oh yeah," she says. "About the joking. Look, I'm sorry, all right? It's not every day one of your best friends pisses her pants while bunking up with the guy she's panting for. Total tease material. Tell me you wouldn't."

"I'm not bunking up with him."

"Whatever. Not exactly flattery, Stace. A few moans would have done the trick."

"You don't know what you're talking about."

"Hey, don't sweat it. I should really be giving you an award for bravery. I think I'd head for Siberia if that happened to me. You just came to the library."

"Thanks," I say, giving up on an explanation for now.

"So are we cool?"

"I guess," I say.

Amber clutches me close like a favorite doll and then pushes me away. "So what's with the piss anyway?"

"It's been happening since the nightmares."

"Freakish."

"Believe me, I'm not too proud of it myself."

"Have you gone to a doctor?"

"Too humiliating. But I went on the Internet. I guess it's fairly common if you have a small bladder."

"Do you?"

"No. Which leads me to believe that in some sick, twisted way, my wetting the bed is my body's way of telling me something."

"And what's it trying to say?"

"Your guess is as good as mine."

"So yucky." She smacks her hand over her mouth and crosses her legs.

"I know."

.   .   .

We leave the library and head to the dorm to meet Drea, the last person on Earth I want to see, never mind work with. It's not every day your best friend makes you feel like some freakish character straight out of a Steven King novel: Stacey Brown, coed by day, psychic bed-wetter by night. Of course, I suppose, it's also not every day one finds their best friend in bed with their ex. I remind myself of this last part all the way through the lobby, down the hallway, and into the room.

Drea is lounging on her bed, one hand propping a chocolate bar up to her bottom lip, the other writing in her diary. She takes a bite and chews over her thought, jotting down her last few words, trying to act as though I'm not important enough to ruffle her.

The sight of her calm little self makes me want to rip the pen right out of her hand and scribble all over her face. I clench my teeth, hearing her voice play over and over again in my head: *Stacey wets the bed. Stacey wets the bed. Stacey wets the bed.*

"Hi Amber," she says, not looking up.

"Hey." Amber brushes by me. She plops herself down on my bed and pauses; "You *did* change the sheets, didn't you?"

Bitch.

"How are we supposed to plan when Veronica's not here?" Amber asks.

"I already called her," Drea says. "She's not coming."

"What do you mean *not coming*?" Amber asks.

"I mean she wants us to leave her alone. She actually thinks *I'm* the one behind all this stalker business."

"You don't just change your mind like that," Amber says.

"It's called being a woman," Drea says. "We have the pre-rogative."

"We need to go there," I say, finally. "We have to convince her."

"Stacey's right," Amber says.

"Fine," Drea says. She caps her pen, gets up, and pockets the chocolate bar in lieu of the protection bottle. "But honestly, I think we're on our own."

twenty-five

It takes a few minutes of knocking and waiting before Veronica actually opens her door. "Can't you take a hint?" she asks, between clenched teeth.

"Not really, Snotty," Amber says, barging her way into the room.

"Excuse me?" Veronica says.

"No sweat." Amber makes herself at home on a fuchsia-pink beanbag chair. "Isn't this the cutest?"

Veronica's room is dripping in shades of pink, making it look like a bedroom straight out of Barbie's dream house.

"I told you guys already," Veronica says. "I'm too old to play Nancy Drew."

"Screw Nancy Drew," Amber says, peering into the magenta telescope by the window. "I want to be a Charlie's Angel."

"Well, you've come to the wrong place." Veronica keeps a hand on the door, waiting for us to leave.

"Look, Veronica," Drea begins, "this isn't exactly my idea of a fun time either, but we need to help each other. You said so yourself."

"Well, I've said a lot of stupid things in my lifetime."

"No doubts there," Amber says.

Veronica flings the door closed. "I already told you. I want nothing to do with this anymore."

"Look, Veronica," I say, "I know you said you think this is all some hoax, but what if it isn't? Don't you think you should take as many precautions as possible? I mean, the guy says he's coming for you tomorrow."

But Veronica doesn't answer. She just stands there, super-rigid, eyes rolled toward the ceiling.

"Wait," Drea says. "What's that?" She takes a couple steps toward Veronica's dresser, her eyes locked on a chunk of white fabric sticking out from the jewelry box.

"What?" Veronica asks.

Drea presses the scalloped trim between her fingers. "This is my handkerchief." She pulls on it, tugging out an extra inch of fabric, revealing the embroidered *D* of her initials. "What's it doing here?" Drea tries pulling up on the lid, but the box is locked.

"What do you *think* it's doing here?" Veronica pulls the key necklace from around her neck to unlock the box. "You gave it to me. Stuffed it inside my mailbox." She dangles the handkerchief over Drea's nose.

"Why would I do that?" Drea snatches it out of Veronica's hand and traces her fingers over the stitched initials, *D. O. E. S.*

"Wait," I say, taking the handkerchief. "This is the same one that got mixed up in the wash when I was doing my laundry, when everything was stolen."

"The laundry was stolen?" Drea asks.

"Yeah. The stalker has your pink bra, by the way."

"Thanks for that image," Amber says.

"The point is, Veronica, that whoever stole the laundry is the one who gave this to you," I say. "Plus, even if it was Drea, why would she go stuffing her things into your mailbox? It would just give her away."

"To tell you the truth," Veronica says, "I have no idea what her logic is. But I want no part of it."

Drea takes the handkerchief back and pats the fabric between her palms. "My mother gave me this on my tenth birthday. I'd never give it up."

"Why should I believe anything any of you has to say?"

"Because, whether you like it or not, Veronica, there's a good chance something's going to happen tomorrow," I say.

"It'll happen tonight, if you don't leave me alone." Veronica rips the handkerchief out of Drea's hands.

"Give it back—now!" Drea moves to snatch it back, but Veronica's too quick. She locks the handkerchief back up in the jewelry box.

"I'm not leaving here without it," Drea says.

"Yes, you will," Veronica's eyes narrow, "because all I have to do is show that to campus police, along with all those letters you've been sending, and get you thrown out of school."

"Can we see the letters?" I ask. "To compare them to Drea's?"

"You can see the door," Veronica says.

"You wouldn't call campus police on us," Drea says, "would you?"

Veronica takes a step forward, landing nose-to-nose with Drea. "You better stop harassing me, Drea Olivia Eleanor Sutton, or I *will*."

twenty-six

Regardless of what Veronica wants, Drea, Amber, and I aren't willing to take any chances. We agree that at least one of us should be with her at all times tomorrow. Drea will be with her in the first three blocks of the day, Amber and I will see her in the fourth and fifth, and then it'll be just me and Ronnie for double-block drama until the bell rings.

After school is a bit more difficult. We end up following her to the Hangman, where she sits at her usual table with Donna, sipping double espressos and doing homework.

"This is so lame." Amber takes a giant gulp of mocha latté, planting a froth mustache over her lip. "She knows what we're doing. It's not like we ever hang out here."

"Who cares?" I break off a piece of scone and pop it into my mouth. "At least we're doing the right thing." I peek at Drea, her posture positioned away from me. "Dray, you want some?"

"No." She grabs a napkin and starts tearing it to shreds.

"Can't we get past this?" I ask. "At least for now? It's not like you didn't completely humiliate me in the cafeteria."

"I'm here for Veronica's sake and mine," she says. "That's it."

"Well, I'm here for your sake too, just in case you forgot." I glance over at Veronica's table. They're packing up and putting on their coats.

"They're out of here," Amber says.

"Then so are we."

We follow Veronica to dinner, sit for two hours in the library during her study group, and then follow her back to her room, where we sit outside in the hall.

"I can't believe we're doing this," Drea says, wiping a stray curl from her face.

"One of us should really be in there with her." I pace the hallway back and forth, getting weird stares from girls on the floor.

"She'll never let us in," Drea says. "We're probably wasting our time. This is probably just some huge joke. It doesn't make sense that someone would stuff *my* hanky in *her* mailbox."

Progress. She's actually talking to me.

"Maybe she's lying," Amber says.

"That's my vote," I say. "She's definitely lying about something."

"What time is it?" Amber whines. "This is torture."

"We only have a couple more hours until midnight," I say, looking at my watch.

"I'd rather die," Drea says.

"Nice choice of words." Amber stomps over to Veronica's door and knocks. "I need grub."

"Are you kidding?" Drea says. "She'll have us arrested."

"It's worth it. I need to snack."

Veronica comes to the door dressed like the burped-out version of her room: a bright-pink turtleneck sweater paired with a short, pink-checked wool skirt. "They told me you were out here."

"Who did?" Amber asks.

"People on the floor."

"Isn't your roommate with you, Veronica?" I peer around her into the room.

"Not that it's any of your business, but Donna had a date tonight. Do you girls even know what a date is?"

"Nice friend," Amber says. "Couldn't she have at least waited until tomorrow? He's not gonna ice you tomorrow."

"For your information, I'm going out too."

"What?" Drea stands up. "You can't go out!"

"Not without us, anyway." Amber places her hands on her hips to block Veronica in.

"You guys don't rule my life. You better be out of here by the time I'm ready to leave, or I'll call campus police." She chases her ungratefulness with a slam of the door.

"We forgot to ask her for grub," Amber whines. "I'm gonna run to the snack machines. You gals want something?"

Drea and I shake our heads, and Amber takes off down the hallway, the paws of her teddy-bear backpack bouncing against her shoulders and hips.

And now it's just me and Drea. Alone.

Several awkward minutes pass. I continue my floor-pacing, anticipating Amber's return. I even calculate the whole snack-trip in my head. Two minutes to walk down to the lobby, three to make a snack selection, and then another two to walk up the stairs.

But luckily Drea breaks the painful silence. "You don't really think Veronica will call campus police on us, do you? She could really pin this all on me, couldn't she?"

"Because of a handkerchief? Please. I think it makes her look guilty that she even has it. Me and Amber are your witnesses. We know it isn't you. Plus, she did cheat on her French test and knows we know about it. Grounds for expulsion."

Drea nods to assure herself.

I feel relieved that she's talking to me again, despite the situation. "How do you think she knew your middle names?"

She stops from biting at her nails to really consider the question. "I don't know. But then, I don't even know how she can think it's me. I mean, I wouldn't exactly be following her around all day, making sure nothing happens to her, if I wanted to hurt her."

So true. "Do you really think she's going out?" I ask.

"I don't know what to think about Veronica anymore," she says.

We spend the next several minutes pacing back and forth, passing each other and memorizing patterns in the speckled gray rug, the kind that never seems to stain. Looking up toward the ceiling at the popcornlike bumps. Waiting for the door to open, for Amber to come back.

Drea looks down at her watch. "It's been, like, an hour. Where the hell is Amber?"

"Maybe one of us should check." But just as the words fall off my tongue, Amber comes bustling through the hallway door, gummy bears and salt-and-vinegar chips in hand. "What took you so long?" I ask.

"Couldn't decide. Then when I did decide, I didn't have money. So, I had to run back to my room, scrounge money out of every jacket in my closet, and then my dad called and I had to talk to him. . . . Gummy bear?"

"No, thanks," I say, turning from her.

Amber presses her ear to Veronica's door, cramming a wad of chips into her mouth. "What did I miss?"

"Nothing," Drea says. "She hasn't even tried to come out."

"It's like church in there," Amber says.

"Maybe she's sleeping," Drea suggests.

I close my eyes and concentrate on the pinks in the room. I try to picture Veronica amidst them, combing her hair, lounging on the bed, or watching TV. I hold the Devic crystal around my neck and rub the point for inspiration, trying to make the image come alive inside my head. But I just can't.

"Stacey, why do you look like you just swallowed a worm?" Amber asks.

"I don't think she's in there."

"Of course she's in there." Drea presses her ear to the door and knocks.

Nothing.

She looks at Amber and me, her lips falling open with a tremble.

"Maybe she fell asleep with her Walkman on," Amber says.

"Or maybe she's not in there," I repeat.

"There's only one way to find out," Drea says. "I can pick the lock."

"You know how?" I ask.

"Since when?" Amber pauses mid-chew.

Drea removes her campus ID card from its plastic holder. She wedges it into the door crack and wiggles it back and forth.

"What do you think you're doing?" says a voice from behind us.

We whirl around to find Becky Allston, class prodigy herself, standing right behind us. She purses her lips and cranes her neck forward to see what we're doing.

"Oh, it's okay," Amber says. "I locked myself out. My friend's just helping me get back in."

Drea fakes a smile and stands in front of the doorknob, like that will make a difference.

"That's not your room," Becky says.

A smart girl.

"I just moved in today," Amber says. "Aren't you gonna, like, welcome me to your floor?" Amber holds her bag of chips out to Becky as an offering.

"No, but I *will* call campus police."

"Go ahead," Amber says, yanking her chips back. "They'll just tell you it's true."

Becky turns on her heels, takes a step back into her room, and slams the door.

"Shit," Amber says, mid-crunch. "We need to bug. It's after eleven anyway."

"No!" Drea turns back to continue with the lock. She swivels her wrist left and right, nuzzling the card in further. "I almost got it." *Click.* Drea smiles. "We're in."

We swing the door wide open and it's just as I expected. Veronica is gone. But she's left two pink suitcases in the middle of the floor.

"So you're telling me she went out the window," Drea says. "That's, like, three stories."

"So doable with a fire escape," Amber says, closing the door and locking it. "Trust me."

"What's with the suitcases?" I ask, checking them out, lifting up on the handle of each to feel the ample weight.

"Maybe she's serious about going home until after this blows over," Drea says.

"Then why would she tell us she thinks it's all fake?"

"Something's screwy," Amber says.

We search around for some clue as to where she might have gone, but her daily planner is empty and her books are still in a pile on the desk.

"She could have gone anywhere," Drea says, trying to unlock the jewelry box with the tip of a pen.

"Bobby pin works better," Amber says, pulling one from behind her ear. "You're not the only one with hidden talents."

I search around Veronica's night table, shuffling through fluorescent-pink sticky notes, wadded-up pink tissue balls, and strawberry Starburst wrappers. Everything looks normal, which makes me feel like we're wasting time, like we should be out looking instead of rifling through nothing.

"Hey guys, look at this." Drea has gotten the jewelry box open. Handkerchief in hand, she plucks out a note, written in the same red block lettering as all the other notes: MIND YOUR OWN BUSINESS.

"What does this mean?" Drea asks.

"It could mean a couple things," I say. "Either someone sent this to Veronica as a warning, maybe because he knew you guys were comparing stalker notes. Or, Veronica wrote it herself and was stashing it away."

"That doesn't make sense," Amber says. "She wouldn't have stashed away her own note. She just would have given it."

"Not unless someone interrupted her and she had to hide it real quick," Drea says.

"I don't know," I say. "But if someone did send this to her, we have to find her—fast."

Amber takes a seat at Veronica's computer table while I weed through Veronica's trash, littering at least a dozen paper balls onto the floor. I smooth each one out against my chest, trying to find some clue as to where she might have gone.

"Hey, *chicas*, check this out." Amber has gotten into Veronica's e-mail. "There's a message from Chad."

Drea and I join Amber at the computer.

"Why would Chad be sending Veronica e-mail?" Drea's jaw tightens.

"Maybe he wants to say good night before bed." Amber smiles in Drea's direction.

We read the message silently to ourselves. *"Dear Veronica,"* it begins. *"Yesterday, after school, I was in Madame Lenore's room and noticed a bunch of cheat sheets in the desk where you sit. I'm pretty sure it's your writing. I was trying to do you a favor by getting rid of them, but when I grabbed them, she came back into the room. I didn't want to get caught with the sheets in my hand, so I hid them in the closest place, along the chalkboard ledge. I know Madame's in there first thing in the morning. If I were you, I'd get them tonight. The window in Room 104 is always open a crack. Good luck. Chad."*

"Why would Chad want to help her?" Drea asks.

"I don't know," I say. "But I bet that's where she is." I touch my Devic crystal and close my eyes. I can picture her there, walking down the main corridor, her heels clanking against the green and white linoleum floor. "Let's go."

"Wait," Drea says. "It doesn't make sense. There's no window left open in 104."

"It's true," Amber says. "Campus police never closes it."

"How do *you* know?"

"I used to date campus police, remember?"

"We don't have time for this," I say. "That's where she is. Let's go."

.   .   .

We leave the room a mess, boog it out the door, and make our way across the muddy soccer field in almost complete darkness. We don't speak to one another, so I have no idea what either of them are thinking. I only know that in my heart there's a sense of dread, and in my belly, the urge to be sick.

Room 104 of the O'Brian Building is just in front of us, the window open a crack, just as Chad's e-mail and Amber said.

"Why didn't we bring a flashlight?" Drea asks.

"I have one." Amber pulls a mini-flashlight from her backpack. She hands it to me. "I never leave home without it."

I aim the light into the classroom, but from what I can see—chalkboards, rows of desks, books under the seats—nothing looks out of the ordinary. "We're gonna have to go in," I say.

"I refuse to go in there," Drea says.

"Why?" Amber asks.

"*Why*? Are you *crazy*? How do I know this isn't some trick? How do I know you guys aren't part of it?"

"What are you talking about?" I ask.

She shakes her head and her mouth tenses into a tight little slit.

"Drea," I say, "you have to come. We're not about to leave you out here alone."

She just keeps shaking her head, sucking in and letting out these enormous breaths, not looking at either of us.

"Drea?"

She blinks hard a few times, as if she can't focus. Her breath quickens, becomes more urgent. She grabs around her throat and starts to hyperventilate. "I can't breathe," she puffs out. Her body begins to waver back and forth. Her feet stumble. "I can't—" But before I have the chance to try and hold her up, she folds to the ground like an old cardboard box.

I squat down by her side. "Amber, do you have your cell phone?" I pull at the backpack resting by Amber's ankles, but Amber snatches it back. "Amber, we need to call campus police."

"We're not supposed to be out here. She'll be okay. She's done this before. Just give her a minute." Amber kneels down and places her hand on Drea's forehead, as though checking her temperature.

"Amber, she doesn't have a fever, give me your phone. *Now!*"

Amber finally gives in and tosses it to me. I try to dial, but nothing happens. I look at the phone screen. "No charge. You need to go for help. I'll stay here."

Amber looks at Drea, gasping for breath; her lips, dry and chalky; her eyes, fluttering closed. She gets up and runs toward the campus road.

I prop Drea's head up on my lap, wondering if I should try CPR. "Help is on the way, Drea. Just hold on."

Drea tries to puff out a few words, but they aren't clear.

"Shh . . . don't try to talk." I wipe the droplets of sweat from her forehead and notice she's cold and shaking as well. I look back up in the direction of the road. Donovan is running toward me. Amber follows close behind, and then Chad.

"What happened?" Donovan drops a spiral sketchbook to the ground, peels off his jacket, and tucks it under Drea's head.

"Amber, didn't you find campus police?"

"I found Donovan first."

"What happened?" Donovan repeats.

"I don't know. She just started hyperventilating."

"I'll go get some help." Chad turns back toward the road.

Donovan's face is sweaty and urgent. He loosens Drea's blouse at the neck and places his hand over her heart. "Come on, Drea," he says. "Try to control your breathing. Don't panic. Breathe in and then blow out."

I can tell Drea is listening to him, relying on the confidence in his voice to help steady her.

"You're still taking too much air into your lungs." Donovan reaches down to hold her sweaty palm. "Try to think about breathing through your chest, in and out. Don't panic. As long as you're breathing, you'll be okay."

It takes Donovan several minutes to calm Drea's breathing. He whips off his sweater, leaving only a thin T-shirt, and covers her with it. "It's okay," he whispers, stroking her hair back. "You're gonna be okay. Just don't try to talk."

"The ambulance is on its way." Chad jogs toward us with a campus police officer.

"She's doing much better." Donovan reaches one arm under Drea's neck and the other at the curve of her back to help her sit up. "She had a panic attack. I used to get them too."

"She's lucky you were here to help," the officer says.

"What were you doing out here, anyway?" I ask.

"I was just sketching." Donovan looks up toward the sky. "When was the last time you saw a sky like tonight?"

I look up, noticing the star formation, the way the waxing moon, still days from first quarter, looks against the inky black sky.

"The best view is from the quad benches, looking north," Donovan continues. "No buildings in the way." He turns to Chad. "Where did you come from?"

"I was just walking across campus. I saw you guys running, and thought maybe something was wrong."

"Normally you'd all get written up for being out after curfew," the officer says. "But all considered, I think we can let a hero and his friends slide."

I'm not even sure Donovan hears him. He's completely soaking on Drea, making sure she's breathing at a normal rate, that her hair is pushed back off her face and her hands aren't dirty from the ground.

"The ambulance is here," I say.

"You'll be all right, Drea." Donovan smiles and rubs her back.

"Don't go, Donovan . . . please." She clasps her hands around his arm, like this is port and he's staying while she's going off to sea. A couple EMTs approach her with a stretcher, but she refuses to look at them until Donovan promises to stay with her.

And suddenly I don't know whether this is reality anymore or if I've been sucked into an episode of *The Young and the Breathless*.

The EMTs make everyone clear the way. Donovan steps back but keeps hold of Drea's hand as she's lifted onto the stretcher.

"I think we should go in the ambulance too," Amber says.

I walk with her toward it, as if I'm going to join them, all the while keeping an eye on the officer as he steps inside his cruiser. "No," I whisper. "You go. One of us should be with her. I need to stay here and check things out."

"Are you *crazy*?" Amber whispers. "Not alone."

I glance at Chad, standing at the back of the ambulance, seeing Drea inside. "I'm not alone."

Amber looks at him. "Are you sure?"

I nod, unsure. "You better go."

Amber lingers a moment more before climbing inside to join Drea and Donovan.

I watch them all go. All except Chad, now standing by my side.

twenty-seven

It's after the ambulance has sped away that I notice Amber left her teddy-bear backpack behind. I pick it up, along with the uncharged cell phone and Donovan's sketchbook, and stuff both inside the bear's belly, already full with Amber's snack machine treats.

"Why didn't you go with Drea?" Chad asks.

"Why didn't you?" I answer. "It's practically midnight, what are you even doing here?"

"I was looking for you. I went to your room. I went to the Hangman. The library—"

"Those things close at eleven."

"Yeah, but I thought maybe you guys were taking your time walking back. What's the big deal?"

I study his face for a prolonged second, trying to decipher the truth, wondering if I should mention his e-mail to Veronica—the whole reason why we're here. "Forget it," I say, finally. I pick up Amber's flashlight and head toward the window.

"What are you doing?"

"You're a smart guy; *you* figure it out." I edge the window open wide enough, hoist myself up on the ledge, belly-first, and crawl my way through the window and onto the classroom floor, my feet landing with a thud.

Chad follows.

I walk past a row of desks, using the flashlight to guide my way. I shine it around the room, in all corners, on the quest for anything that appears unclassroomlike. But, aside from the lack of lighting and the obvious vacancy of the place, it's just like any other classroom I've ever sat in— needlessly oppressive and completely stagnant.

"What are we doing?" Chad whispers.

I shush him with a finger and approach the front of the room. Sprawled across the chalkboard are the notes from the day's trig lesson, something about the l of m, and someone's left their biology books in the basket under the chair. My flashlight beam passes over the light switch by the door. But I don't want to flip it on, just in case campus police are still lurking.

I move over to the door and wrap my hand around the knob, feeling a cold rush of blood run from my face. I whip the door open, causing it to crash against the wall and the trash can to topple onto the floor. My heart makes a bungee-cord jump into my belly and then up to my throat before snapping back into place.

Chad picks the trash can up and looks at me—his face blurred by the darkness. "Are you okay?" He places his hand at my forearm. That's when reality really hits, reminding me where I am and what I'm doing. I pull my arm away and step out onto the green and white checkerboard floor, heading in the direction of Madame Lenore's French room.

The flashlight beam paves about a three-yard distance in front of me. The rest is black. I shout Veronica's name a couple times, my voice echoing off the walls. I actually want her to be here—to be waiting for me, to be playing some trick, it doesn't really matter—because right now, even with Chad, I feel completely alone.

I focus on the red exit sign at the end of the hall, just to the left of the French room. The idea of it, of booting it out of here, keeps me moving forward, further down the hall-way, further away from Chad, if he's still following behind me.

When the beam of the flashlight is close enough to illuminate the exit door, I stop, my eyes lodged on the handles. It can't be true. It can't be real. But it is. I blink at least a dozen times, but it still is. A thick metal chain is threaded through and around both handles. If I want to get out, I'll have to backtrack.

I stand there a moment, trying to decide whether or not this is really worth it. Maybe I should just forget it. Maybe I can tell Drea and Amber that I checked everything out, that Veronica was nowhere in sight, and just turn around and leave.

But it's too late for that.

I make my way past the Hillcrest trophy case, noticing for the first time that all the classroom doors have been closed.

All except for the French room.

"Veronica?" I call toward the open door, still not quite close enough to see inside.

I hold the flashlight with trembling hands as I stall, scanning over banners rooting for Hillcrest's Hornets, posters for class president, and dropped pencils.

"Stacey?" says a male voice. Chad's voice. I'm sure of it.

"Chad?" I turn around to find him, but the slender beam of the flashlight won't let me see far enough. "Where are you? I can't see you."

"I'm right here."

But with the echo in the hallway, I can't quite tell if his voice is coming from in front or behind me.

I wait several seconds for him to say something else. But when he doesn't, I keep moving closer toward the open French room, a spattering of tears rolling down my face before I even go in.

And when I do, I find her.

Veronica.

She's lying on the ground, a collection of textbooks surrounding her head, as well as Madame Lenore's clay planter, still in one piece. There's a narrow stream of liquid running from her head, pooling itself into a pear-shaped puddle. I shake my head over and over again, swallowing the bile down, telling myself that the running liquid is just a water spill from the planter or a leak from the ceiling.

But I know it's really blood. That she's dead. Her moss-green eyes stare up at me, wide open and disappointed, asking me why I didn't get here sooner.

I glance up toward the window shade, slapping against the wooden ledge. The chilly November air filters into the classroom, plays with the wisps of cinnamon-brown hair at the base of her forehead, now stained bright Valentine red. I cover my face with my hands. That's when the darkness in the room folds in and swirls all around me. When my body hits the floor.

twenty-eight

The blare of the phone ringing startles me out of sleep. I spring up to a seated position. For a few confused moments, I think maybe last night was just a horrible nightmare. I look over at Drea's empty bed. My first thought is that she's in class, that I slept through the alarm clock and missed first period. But then it dawns on me that it's Saturday, four lilies later.

Drea's day to die.

"Hello?"

"Stacey, hi, it's me, Chad. How are you?"

"How do you think?"

"Well, how are you feeling, at least?"

"Like I told the police last night, I'm fine. It was more of a shock than anything else."

I close my eyes and try to paste the pieces of last night together in my mind. I remember passing out, being walked to a police car, and all the flashing lights. The smell of eucalyptus and lemon oils stuffed up my nose. Voices trying to talk to me, asking me if I was okay. "Yes, fine," I assured them.

"Do you want to call home?" they asked. "Do you need a doctor?"

"No. I just want to go back to the dorm and sleep."

I remember being hysterical—crying, then laughing, and crying again. How someone, a school nurse maybe, told the police I needed to get some rest. And then how the police said they were going to keep an eye on me and talk to me in the morning. *This* morning. Even though it's already after eleven.

But most of all, I remember Veronica, lying dead in the classroom, her haunting green eyes staring up at me, disappointed.

"They think I did it," Chad said. "They think I killed her."

"What are you talking about?"

"When I came into the classroom, I saw Veronica and I saw you, and I knew you had fainted. So I tried to help you, but then it occurred to me that maybe I should go to the window, you know, to see if I could see anything, catch whoever did it. And then the police came in and saw me and thought I was trying to escape. And then they saw you, just lying there. And Veronica . . . they thought right away that I did it. They asked me what happened. I started telling them, you know, how I saw you guys helping Drea, and then how I followed you into the school. Then they stopped me and read me my rights. They made me call my parents."

"What did your parents say?"

"They told me to cooperate, to just tell them everything. So I did. The police questioned me for over an hour. First one guy, then this lady. Then back and forth. My parents ended up getting a flight here first thing this morning. They're pissed. They're hiring a lawyer."

I think I hear a slight whimper in his voice, where his breath can't quite catch up to the words.

"I gotta go," he says. "I just wanted to make sure you were all right."

"Chad?"

"Just tell me you don't think I'm guilty, Stace. I really need someone to believe me right now."

I don't say anything right away; I just listen to his breath on the other end. "I do believe you," I say, finally, quickly, not knowing if I really do. The phone makes a clicking sound on the other end. "Chad?" But he's already hung up and I have no idea if he even heard me.

I'm just about to call him back when I notice Amber's teddy-bear backpack sitting on the floor beside my bed. The police must have thought it was mine. I pick it up and unzip the belly. Donovan's mini-sketchbook sits at the top. I pull it out and stuff it into the inside pocket of my jacket, wondering if he's still with Drea at the hospital, if I'll see him there. Then I pluck out Amber's cell phone, still dead, and plug the charger into the outlet behind my bed.

I grab the phone to call Drea at the hospital, but hear a jingling sound outside the door. Maybe that's her now. I creep toward the edge of the bed, noticing that the crack of hallway-light at the bottom of the door has been blocked— like someone's standing there.

I place the phone back down on its cradle and get up slowly, watching the dark shadows play at the bottom of the door. From the center of the room, I wait several seconds for a knock or for someone to enter. When neither happens, I yank the baseball bat from the corner and, in one quick motion, whip the door open.

Freaking Amber. She's scribbling a note on the message board attached to the door.

"What is wrong with you?" I say. "You scared the crap out of me."

"Some good morning," she says, inviting herself in. "I guess I don't need to ask how you're doing." Amber closes the door behind her. "I heard about what happened. I can't believe Veronica's dead."

"Believe it. Because it's true."

"I know," she says, fingering along the windowsill, staring out toward the lawn. "It's just that . . . that wasn't supposed to happen, you know?"

I reach into the spell drawer for my bottle of lavender, hoping the floral scent will help soothe my spirit.

"I heard they're canceling classes for next week," Amber says. "There's supposed to be some assembly about it later, but everybody's leaving for the weekend." She watches me dab fingerprints of the oil behind my ears. "Are you all right? You seem a bit distracted."

"How do you *think* I am? Veronica Leeman was lying dead in front of me just a few hours ago and you have as much remorse about it as a chipped pedicure."

"Why should I have remorse? I didn't do it. I mean, yeah, I feel bad—I may not have liked her, but I didn't want her to *die*."

I cap the bottle and pop it back inside the drawer. There's really no sense pursuing this topic any further with her because if I do, I may very well go ballistic and today, of all days, I need to remain calm. Strength comes with mindfulness.

"Did Drea spend the night at the hospital?" I ask finally.

"What are you talking about? Isn't she with you?"

"Why would she be with me?"

"I dropped her off here last night. After the hospital."

"What do you mean, you dropped her off?"

"Yeah, after she called her parents and got checked out, I called PJ to come and pick us up. He did and we dropped her off here."

I look at Drea's bed, the covers still very much intact. "You couldn't have. She didn't come home last night."

"I think I'd know if we dropped her off or not."

"Who's 'we'?"

"I told you. Me and PJ."

"What happened to Donovan?"

"He took a cab back. PJ got all piss-jealous of Donovan, saying I was hanging all over him, which I wasn't. So, then, Donovan had to take a cab back because PJ didn't want him in his car."

"So what about Drea? What happened when you dropped her off?"

"Yeah, so we drove back to campus, and I told PJ to wait in the car for me while I walked Drea into the lobby. I needed some time alone with him, to tell him off. He can't keep thinking of me as his juice."

"So you never actually walked Drea up here?"

"No."

Our eyes lock. Regardless of what roles Amber and I play in this whole ordeal, we both know that this means—today is Drea's day to die and she's already missing.

There's a knock at the door. "Ms. Brown?" says the female voice from the hallway.

Amber and I look at the door, then at each other. "Piglets," Amber whispers. "I refuse to talk to them. We don't have to, you know. We're minors." She snatches her teddy-bear backpack from my bed and heads to the window.

"*Wait!*" I hiss. "What do you think you're doing?"

"Leaving. If you're smart you'll do the same." Amber opens the window and straddles one leg over the sill.

"*Are you crazy?*" I grab at her arm. "You can't leave now. You need to tell them about last night. About Drea. *Remember? Drea?*"

Amber hesitates a moment, but then pulls her arm away. "I can't. Talking to police totally freaks me out, Stace. They make you feel guilty."

"Not if you're innocent."

She looks away. "Call me as soon as she leaves. Don't worry, Stace. We'll get to the bottom of this."

At that, she flips her other leg over the sill and runs across the lawn, toward the forest.

twenty-nine

I throw the door open only to find a short, fragile-looking woman standing in front of me, head to toe in a black DKNY-ish suit, snug cream blouse underneath, and shiny black ankle boots with a square toe.

"Hi," she says, in a voice as petite as she is. "Are you Stacey Brown?"

I nod.

She introduces herself as Officer Tate, though it might as well be Tart because that's exactly what she looks like—

twenty-something, shoulder-length, artfully highlighted ginger-brown hair, with a chunk of platinum that dangles over one eye. "I have a few questions to ask you about last night," she says, flashing me her badge. "Can I come in?"

I nod and step aside, allowing tart-woman to find her place in the center of the room. She pulls a thin spiral notebook from a square, shiny black purse and flips to a fresh page. But, since we're hardly talking manicures here, before she can even *try* to take control of the situation, I grab a firm hold of the reins. "I have a few questions too." I toss the door closed. "My roommate is missing and I want to know what you're going to do about it."

She studies my expression from behind two bright, aqua-colored contacts, waiting for my stare to break, for me to look away. When I don't, she pulls the pencil from behind a double-pierced ear and places it against the clean, white notebook page.

"How long has she been missing?"

"Since last night. She was dropped off here, in front of the dorm, but then never made it back to her room."

"Might there be a chance she's staying in someone else's room? Have you two been fighting?"

"No. I mean yes. I mean, yes, we did get into a fight. But no, she wouldn't have stayed in someone else's room."

"How do you know?"

"Look, I don't have time to argue. I just know."

"You're not helping me here, Stacey."

"Didn't you hear me?" I ask. *"Drea's in trouble."*

"I need you to calm down." She motions to the bed for me to sit. But how can I? How am I supposed to relax when Drea is missing and I'm the only one who seems to care? I grab the protection bottle from the night table and hold it into my chest.

"Look, Stacey, we can talk in circles and get nothing accomplished, or you can let me help you. But the only way I can do that is if you talk to me. Start from the beginning and tell me what happened."

"Fine," I say, even though this whole scenario of having to start from the beginning with little Miss Clairol, who doesn't seem to be the least bit interested in Drea, is so completely un-fine.

"Good." She hands me the glass of water by the bed. "Have you talked to your parents about this yet?"

I shake my head.

"Well, I need you to talk to them before I question you."

"Why? My mother won't care."

"It's just procedure. You need to tell her the situation and that you're going to talk to me. I can't question you unless you do." She pulls out a cell phone. "What's your mother's number?"

I roll my eyes and rattle off the number, thinking how completely senseless this formality is. How completely senseless that my teenie-bop-wannabe mom has been granted the title of adult, while I am still considered a child.

"Hello? Mrs. Brown? This is Officer Jan Tate of the Hanover Police Department. Your daughter, Stacey, would like to speak to you." Officer Tate extends the phone to me. I take and place it up to my ear.

"Stacey," my mother says, "what's going on?"

"Mom, something bad happened. A girl on campus was murdered last night and I . . . found the body."

"What?"

"I know. I'm going to talk to the police about it. I just needed to tell you first."

"Stacey, wait. Why are they questioning you? Why didn't you call me about this last night? You're not in any kind of trouble, are you?"

"I don't know," I say.

"Is Drea being questioned, too?"

"No, Drea is missing."

"*Missing?* What do you mean, missing?" she asks.

"I mean I can't find her and I don't know where she is."

"Oh my god, Stacey. Do you need me to come up?"

I spend the next several seconds trying to convince my mother that I can handle the situation on my own, but she makes me promise to call her back after talking to the tart-lady anyway.

I hang up and look over at Officer Tate, busy eyeing the chunky crystal rock and assortment of candles on my night table. "Okay," I say, breaking her glance. "All set."

.   .   .

Since I can't bear sticking my feet into the muddied-up shoes from last night, still completely soaked from our jaunt across the wet soccer field, and since I can't locate two matching shoes amidst all the clothing debris in our room, I have no choice but to pull out the yellow tennis sneakers from my closet, the ones with the thick wooden beads on the laces. The ones from my nightmare.

I stuff the protection bottle into my coat pocket and follow her out the lobby door, keeping pace at least three steps behind. Luckily, she parked the cruiser in the side lot where there isn't a lot of people-traffic. I ride in the back seat, even though she grants me the privilege of sitting in the front, and keep my head low so no one will see me.

When we get there, Officer Tate leads me into the station—a bit different than what it looks like in the movies. Instead of desks lined up in neat school-rows, ink blotters littered with glazed doughnuts and Styrofoam cups, and phones ringing off the hook, it's pin-drop quiet. A dark piece of glass separates the reception room from the offices. Officer Tate nods to the guy behind the window and he buzzes us through.

I follow her down a short corridor, taking the opportunity to peek into the offices that branch off on both sides, at the officers working on computers and rummaging through files. She points to the room on the right. "Have a seat in there and I'll be right with you."

Here's where it looks like TV. Stark white walls, dusty linoleum floor, laminated-wood table, and metal folding chairs. I pluck the protection bottle from my pocket and grip it in my palm for strength.

Officer Tate comes in shortly after. She closes the door behind her and places a tape recorder on the table between us. We sit down; she smiles at me, pushes record, and we just start talking. We talk about Veronica and the details of the night before. She makes me go over every detail, from the moment we broke into Veronica's room to when I found her body in the classroom. I quickly realize that Miss Clairol is a lot smarter than her hairdo might profess. She twists and turns her questions to try and trip me up, get me to say something different. But I know all the answers; I'm confident about them. And I don't have anything to hide. *Almost.*

"Did you happen to see who sent the e-mail?" She studies my face for an answer.

I look down toward the protection bottle in my lap, wondering what I'm doing, why I'm trying to protect him.

"It was from Chad," I say finally, feeling selfish for not saying so in the first place.

She nods as though she already knows. "In your opinion, Stacey, were Chad and Veronica very good friends?"

I shake my head, knowing exactly where this line of questioning is headed.

"So, why do you think he would be so concerned about her cheating?"

I shrug.

"Do you think there's a chance he just wanted to be alone with her?"

"No." I mask my hand up over my eyes at the thought of Chad asking her there and then showing up only a little while after. "Why would he?"

"Do you need a minute?"

I shake my head and take a deep breath. "I don't know why he would do that."

When Officer Tate appears satisfied enough with my answers, she ends up humoring me for several more minutes while I unload about my nightmares and the card reading. The phone calls, notes, missing laundry, the lilies and what they mean—the way I was able to sense the smell of dirt from their stems and petals. I tell her how I've sensed the smell of dirt before, from Drea's pink bra, and how I was able to feel its vibrations in the laundry room. I even tell her how I've been trying to help Drea with my spells. How Amber, Drea, and I created the protection bottle and then consecrated its powers. And when I'm done, when I'm finally able to take a breath, she looks at me as though I'm crazy, as though *I* should be the one going to a hospital.

Of course, none of what I say—not one single syllable—does she deem notebook-worthy. And this alone makes me want to rip the damn notebook out of her prettily paraffin-ed hands and chuck it in the trash.

"Do you still have any of the notes that Drea received?" she asks.

I shake my head, remembering how Drea burned the notes over one of my candles. But then I remember. "We did find a note in Veronica's jewelry box."

"What did it say?

"'Mind your own business.'"

"Hmm . . . sounds like maybe someone was angry at Veronica."

"Obviously," I say.

"Listen, Stacey," she says with a big sigh, then leans forward, resting her elbows on the table. "Let's say that Drea *did* receive those things. It's hard to follow a lead like that without any evidence."

"Isn't Veronica Leeman's body evidence enough?"

"Let's talk about that. Amber told me you girls went to the school last night to get a book you left in one of the rooms."

"She did? When did you talk to *her*?"

Officer Tate clears her throat, ignoring the question. "From what you just told me, that obviously isn't true."

I consider compromising the truth in some way. Some way to support all the information I just gave her and protect Amber's lie at the same time. I turn to glance at the door, wondering if it's locked, why there aren't any windows in this room. Why it's so freakishly hot.

"No," I say, deciding on the truth.

"Do you know why Amber might have lied?"

I shake my head. Sure, it might have something to do with not getting caught for breaking into somebody's room, being out after curfew, or breaking in and trespassing on school property. But the penalty for those things seems so incredibly minor compared to what's already happened. Amber doesn't have a right to lie. And neither do I.

"I'll tell you what," she begins, "I'll make a report about your roommate's alleged disappearance and check into it personally. But first, I need you to answer something for me. Have you ever talked to anyone about all these visions you say you have?"

"What do you mean, 'visions I *say* I have'?"

"Well, Stacey, you have to admit, it's not exactly . . . common."

I stand up from the table, air sucking up into my lungs, sending my voice three octaves higher. *"You don't believe me?"*

"I didn't say that."

"Look, whether you think I'm crazy or not, someone's after Drea." I hold the protection bottle up to my head, where it's begun to ache. "Don't you understand? He's going to kill her, just like he killed Veronica. The cards, the lilies, the notes, my nightmares . . . today is Drea's day to die."

Officer Tate stands up from the table, her voice like powdery beach sand. "I think you need to get some more rest. You had a pretty unsettling night last night. That would make anybody a bit . . . confused." She presses the stop button on the recorder.

"I'm not confused!"

She pulls a business card from her jacket pocket and holds it out like a lollipop, like she's the nurse and I'm the patient and this is a pediatrician's office.

Like nothing I've said means anything.

"I'll probably need to ask you more questions later," she says. "But call me if you think of anything else."

"So, you're going to look for Drea?" I ask.

"As I said, I'll look into it and get back to you. But don't worry, she probably stayed in someone else's room, especially if you girls were fighting. We see this type of thing all the time." She gestures once more for me to take her card. I slip it into my back pocket.

"Good." She smiles. "Now, let me give you a ride back to campus." She holds the door open wide for me to leave.

That's when I know for sure. If I want to save Drea, I'll have to do it myself.

thirty

The trek across the Hillcrest campus to the boys' dorms takes longer than usual. The police have blocked off the entire O'Brian Building, including the parking lot and quad area in front of it, forcing students onto the main walkways. News teams, school administrators, and curious spectators flock to the scene, eager to feast upon any juicy tidbits that aren't being served up on the morning news. Lucky for me the story is still relatively fresh; news reports are still referring to me as "the female student who found the body." Still, I have to wonder if any of them know it's me.

I scurry through packs of students as best I can, dodging suitcases and shifting knapsacks—people escaping for the weekend. Some senior boys are treating this like a cheesy horror movie, running around, making sick jokes, trying to get people more riled up, if that's even possible. "Last one off campus is a dead coed," one of them shouts.

Meanwhile, a group of freshman girls stands in a huddle only a few yards away, crying and hugging each other. I lock eyes with one of them—a girl with spiky red hair and a freckly face. Her lips part when she spots me, and I wonder if that's suspicion crawling across her face. I look away and keep on going.

When I feel it's somewhat safe, I stop to look closer at the scene. The O'Brian Building looks so different from last night, so violated, with its yellow police tape and swarm of photographers. My eyes wander around the individual faces—crying, shaking, gesturing toward the open window where we entered.

I'm just about to turn away when I see Veronica. She's standing beyond the yellow tape, her face positioned toward me, resting over the shoulder of a much older man, in an embrace.

I blink a few times in confusion, with excitement, thinking for just a moment that somehow, in some way, this has all been a huge mistake.

But then I see it's not Veronica at all.

The woman breaks the embrace, but keeps her arm tucked into the man's side as she continues to sob into the collar of his jacket. Her hair hangs down to the tops of her shoulders, curly and brownish, the color of nutmeg. But it's her eyes that startle me the most. Unmistakable, doelike and mossy green. Veronica's eyes. Veronica's mother.

The sight of her makes my knees tremble, my heart squelch. I felt terrible before. Horrible. Guilty. Responsible. But seeing Veronica as someone's lost daughter makes it so much worse.

I continue across campus, tunneling my vision, trying not to focus on any one person or thing. The ironic part of this whole police/security scene is that when I get to the boys' dorm, there's no one working the front desk, just fleets of boys filtering through the exit doors, not even signing out for the weekend. I thread my way past them and climb up the stairs to the second floor. I need to find the one person who I think can solve this riddle.

PJ.

"Yeah," he says, peeking through the door crack.

"PJ?" It's so dark in his room I can barely make out his face. "Is that you?"

"Who else would it be?" He ekes the door open a bit wider, enabling me to see that he's dyed his hair yet again. This time, jet black.

"What's with the dark room?" I push him out of the way and step inside.

"Helps me think. I like to do that from time to time." He closes the door behind me. "Pretty crazy out there. A little too real for me."

"Unreal," I whisper. I look toward the window at the shade, drawn down, and wonder why he insists on keeping us in the dark. "I almost didn't recognize you with your hair that color."

"Might you have mistaken me for this month's cover of *GQ*?" He palms the tips of his hair spikes, but it isn't with his usual flair. He isn't smiling, isn't bursting with confidence. And he isn't even really looking at me.

"Mightn't," I say, flipping the light switch up.

He squints. "To what do I owe such joyance?"

"We need to talk."

"Sounds cereal."

"It is. I need you to tell me exactly what happened last night when you picked Drea and Amber up at the hospital."

"What do you mean? I picked them up and dropped them off."

"You dropped both of them off?"

"Si, Senorita."

"Amber told me she walked Drea into the lobby and then went back to your car to talk."

"Yeah, right. She wanted to be alone with me. Who could blame her? Little vixen."

"You two weren't fighting?"

"Fighting? Quite the contrary. Unless you call love bites injurious."

"No," I argue. "You two were fighting. You were mad at her. About Donovan. About how she was hanging all over him. Ignoring you."

"You're speaking a totally different language here. I don't know what you're talking about. Amber can PB-and-jam with whomever she wants, including me when she cares to. Last night in point."

My head starts spinning. I throw my hands up over my face to try and stop it. "I need to sit down."

PJ gestures to his bed, littered with dirty laundry and old pizza boxes. I navigate a clear spot and plunk down. "You want some *agua*?" He reaches into his mini-fridge and passes me a gallon jug, the spout christened with chocolate mouth stains. I take a sip anyway. "What's going on with you?" he asks. "Is it Veronica?"

I nod. "And, like that isn't bad enough, Drea's missing. She never made it back to the room after you dropped her off last night."

"That's impossible. Maybe she just went out before you got up this morning."

I can't bear to listen to any more plausible explanations for Drea's whereabouts. I wrestle myself up from the hovel of his bed. "Can you just answer me one more question?"

"What?"

"How long was Amber in the lobby with Drea before she came back to your car?"

"I don't know, like, five minutes. Not enough time to kill anybody."

"Why would you say that?" I snap. "How can you even—?"

"Look, Stace," he says, "you're getting a bit weird here, even for me. You're talking all wiggy. I'm sure Drea is fine. Probably getting her nails filled at some spa. Why don't you go to the police and dog them about it? There's enough of them crawling around here." He inches the window shade to peek outside. "I've got my own doo-doo to deal with today."

"Like what?" I ask.

"Like not having an alibi for last night."

"Why would you need one? Where were you?"

"Here. Dyeing my hair. Thought with Amber falling all over Donovan, she'd appreciate my new, sultry look—tall, dark, and dangerously dashing."

"I thought you didn't care who she flirted with."

"I don't," he says.

"So why do you need an alibi?"

"Because I hated Veronica Leeman and maybe a part of me wanted her to croak. You know it. Everybody knows it. And people are starting to talk about it."

"What people?"

"It doesn't matter. What matters is that nobody saw me around the dorm last night and no one was at the desk to check me in."

"Now *you're* the one who's talking wiggy."

"Maybe," he says, opening the door to let me out. "Or maybe I *am* wiggy."

thirty-one

Not knowing where to go or what to think, I head back to my room. But before I can even venture a toe inside I'm stopped by the hairy-faced wonder herself: Madame Discharge.

"You missed the assembly," she says.

"I know. I had to go off campus." I stick my key into the lock and avoid eye contact, hoping she gets the picture.

"It wasn't a voluntary assembly. You were marked absent. You had to get special permission from a parent or guardian to miss."

I turn the key. *Click.* I'm in. Now why won't she go away? I look up at her, hoping to pacify her curiosity enough so she'll leave. "I'm sorry. I'll be sure to go and apologize to Principal Pressman first chance I get."

She takes a step closer and I can smell the snacks on her breath—Doritoes mixed with Diet Coke. She studies my face—the way my eyes move, the involuntary puffing of my cheeks. "When they called you absent, some girls said they saw you get into a police car. Is that true?"

I shake my head, slip into my room, and close the door. I hardly have time to worry about Madame Discharge or anyone else who might be spreading stuff about me. It's almost five. Only seven hours left before midnight, when the day is completely over. I plop down on my bed and notice Amber's cell phone sticking out by my feet. I unplug it from its charger and stuff it into my pocket, thinking how Amber lied to me about talking to Officer Tate, how I haven't heard from her since this morning.

It doesn't make sense and I can't think anymore. I pull Officer Tate's card from my back pocket and dial. Maybe she's discovered something about Drea.

"Hello?" I say. "I need to speak to Officer Tate. Tell her it's Stacey Brown."

But Officer Tate isn't in and I don't bother leaving a message. I try calling my mother back as promised, thinking how maybe a little maternal inspiration might do me good right about now, but the phone just rings and rings. Great.

I reach for the family scrapbook. If I can't communicate with the spirit world in my sleep, I'll do it during my waking hours. I flip to the section labeled Channeling Spirits and decide to do the spell written by my great-grandmother.

The spell directions indicate that you're supposed to make the letters of the alphabet by cutting up sheets of paper and writing on them. But there isn't time. I reach up into my closet and pull the dusty Scrabble game from the top shelf. I've had it since my fourth-grade spelling bee and know some of the letters are missing, but it doesn't matter. I'm confident it will do just fine.

I push my bed to the side to make room for a sacred circle, place eight thick, white candles on the floor, marking all the directions north to west, and light them with a long, wooden match. My grandmother always stressed the importance of a solid circle, one that can't be penetrated by unrested spirits looking for an opening.

I sprinkle Kosher salt and sugar around the perimeter of the circle and place stones and crystals around the edges. Into the middle, I set a freshly washed ceramic bowl. And to it, I add a few bits of chocolate from the bar Drea was eating last night (the bits with the tooth-mark impressions), a wad of hair from her brush, and the couple of bitten fingernail shards (still attached to the acrylic) that I'm able to find in the trash.

I spread the Scrabble tiles out in front of me, placing the Y tile to the left for yes, the N tile to the right for no, and the Q tile above to stand for the question mark. Everything's ready. I sit in silence for many moments, trying to gain equilibrium with the energies that flow through my body and the room. "Evil is not allowed to enter this sacred circle," I whisper. "This sacred circle is safe. This sacred circle is powerful. And this sacred circle is all-telling. I imagine a circle of light above this sacred circle. It surrounds me and keeps me safe as I invoke the powers that be to allow me to speak to those who have passed on."

The temperature in the room drops and a shiver runs over my shoulders. "Sacred Mother, I invoke thee to let me speak to Anne Blake, my grandmother." I position my hands over the letters and wait for many moments, for the windows to rattle or the floor to shake—all the invented stories you hear about late-night Ouiji-board adventures and slumber party séances. But nothing like that happens. In fact, the room seems quieter than ever.

I close my eyes again and concentrate even harder. "Grandma?" I whisper. "Are you here?" I rotate my hands, palms down, counterclockwise over the letters. That's when I feel the energy in the room guide my fingers toward the Y tile.

"Can you help me make sense of my nightmares?" I feel my hands draw toward the Q tile. I take a deep breath in to try and quiet the questions that fly through my brain, and end up asking the most obvious question of all: "Do you know who Drea's stalker is?" My hands move to the Y tile.

I take another deep breath, preparing myself for the answer. I almost don't want to know. "What is his name?" I ask.

I wait for several seconds, for the energy to swim through my fingers and guide me toward the answer. I rotate my hands over the letters and bend my wrists up and down, like that will make a difference. But it's almost as if my grandmother can help, but only if I figure things out for myself.

"Is the stalker someone I know?" My hands stop mid-rotation and move to the Y.

I close my eyes, concentrating on what I should ask next, and the question seems obvious. "Why am I having these nightmares?" I feel drawn into the letters, my fingers moving into the pool, extracting the tiles that feel right. I shift them all around until the energy in my hands rests, until the letters spell out TEL FUTR. I don't have time to dwell on the missing Scrabble pieces. I have to keep going.

I push the tiles back into the pool and return my hands to hovering-position. "The stalker said that he'd come for her. Now that he has, where has he taken her?" I feel the energy guide my fingers back into the letters, choosing a series of tiles and sliding them into place. This time they spell out YR DREMS.

I think about it a few moments. If my dreams are supposed to help me tell the future, then the answer to where I will find Drea is somewhere inside them. It makes perfect sense, like I've known all along.

I watch the candle flames waver back and forth like tiny glowing snakes, wondering if I should ask my other question, if it will help me, if there's time. "Grandma," I whisper, "why have I been wetting the bed? What does it mean?"

The room grows colder in the few seconds that I wait. I keep my eyes closed, concentrating on the question, confident in my thoughts. After a few moments, it feels as though the energy has taken hold of my hands. My fingers grab at the letters, plucking out a handful and arranging them into place. They spell out S HDN.

S Hdn? What's that supposed to mean?

I don't have time to stop and figure it out. I have to trust what I already know. "Thank you, Grandma," I whisper. "I miss you." I extinguish the candles with the snuffer to end the séance, and step out of the sacred circle. I head to where I know I'll find Drea.

The forest.

thirty-two

I enter the forest through the tree-lined opening behind our dorm. Before I leave, I end up calling Officer Tate to tell her where I'm going. Whether or not she takes me seriously is a completely different story.

Still, she says she'll come. I pray she will.

It's dark; the webbing of branches above me blocks out any remaining light from the falling sun. It will probably be less than an hour before I won't be able to see anything at all. Why didn't I think to bring a flashlight?

The smell of earth surrounds me and seems to intensify with each careful step. I walk for several minutes, doing my best to stay on some sort of path, to keep moving in a forward direction. I concentrate on the sounds around me—crickets chirping, leaves rustling, and twigs snapping beneath my feet. But then I hear something else—footsteps maybe, the sound of someone's body moving through the brush, scraping against the branches.

I try to decipher what direction it's coming from, but the ringing in my pocket stops me, sends a trickle of panic down the bones of my spine. Amber's cell phone. I forgot I even had it. I squat down behind a tree to answer it. "Hello?"

"Stacey, thank god you have my phone."

"Amber?" I whisper. "I can't talk right now."

"Meet me in my room. I've decided I want to talk to the police."

"You've already talked to them; I know you have."

"I talked with some cop lady for, like, five minutes. But then I completely freaked and pulled a chew-and-screw, only it was a talk-and-screw, and booged it out of there. So, I didn't really say much. What can I say? I've gone from denial to separation to totally wigging in less than twenty-four hours. Murder has that effect on me, I guess. It's so *Heathers* and *The Craft*, you know? Real."

"I'm a little busy," I say.

"Well, *unbusy* yourself because I'm ready to talk to the police *now*, Stacey, and I want you to be here when I do."

"*I can't!*"

"You can and you will. It's for Drea. I'll see you in a few minutes." She hangs up.

I hang up too, with no intentions of going to meet her. I just don't have any more time to waste.

I continue on my path, concentrating on the essence of the forest, hoping it will bring me to Drea. It's quiet again, as if whoever was following me stopped or went in another direction.

A couple more minutes along, I reach a partial clearing. I look up at the sky for some sort of direction, as though the dark clouds can part the way, open up to some sort of fold-out map. But they've gathered up into a smoky-blue cluster of lilies, reminding me that I need to hurry.

I take giant steps with my arms outstretched, swiping brush from in front of my face. I stop a moment and turn, sure that someone is moving behind me again. I take a few quick steps to create a distance. The person following does the same.

I speed up even more—running now—doing my best to weave through the brush and find a place to hide. The ground is turning to sludge beneath my feet. With each step it gets deeper, slowing me down, pulling at my sneakers.

I take a big step and my foot sinks, beyond ankle-deep, into the mud. I pull up on my leg. The weight of the mud literally swallows up my sneaker. Barefoot now, I struggle to trudge my way through the sopping muck, to reach steadier ground. But then I have to stop. There's a gnaw-ing ache in the arch of my one bare foot. The feeling ex-plodes toward my ankle and up my leg. I reach down to feel the spot. There's a stick poking out through my skin.

I feel myself begin to pant; feel the lights behind my eyes go dim. I want to be sick. I reach out into the darkness for a branch to help steady me, but end up slipping, smacking down against the cold, wet earth.

"Stacey?" whispers a male voice.

It's different than the one I expect to hear—smoother, gentler. Sincere. Still, I scrounge a rock from the ground, feel for its roughest edge, and ready myself for attack.

"Stacey?" the voice repeats. "Is that you?"

A beam of light finds its way from my bare foot to my face, making me squint. And then it moves to highlight his.

It's Donovan. And he's hiding. He's squatted himself down between two wiry shrubs, his face partially covered by a web of branches.

"Are they gone?" he asks. "Did you see anyone?" His face is pale, masked in a mix of fear and sweat.

But what is he doing here?

I shake my head and grab at my bare foot, trying to assess how deep the stick went in—a half-inch, maybe.

"What happened?" he asks.

But I'm panting too hard, perspiration dripping from my temples, that I don't answer.

Donovan pulls a cell phone from his pocket. He dials and places the phone up to his ear. "Shit," he says.

"What?" I mutter.

"Nine-one-one. I've been trying to call but can't get reception on my cell." He looks over both shoulders, parts a web of branches, and moves toward me. He zooms the flashlight on my foot. "Here, let me help you." He places the flashlight on the ground so that the beam remains angled at my foot. The stick punctured right through the fabric of my sock, right through the bandage I used to tape up the cut I got from the broken window glass in our room. Donovan surveys the wound and then takes the end of the stick.

"Slowly," I say, giving him permission.

He nods and twists the stick ever so carefully, working it out from my arch. I flinch a couple times as it's pulled out completely, imagining how it must have punctured the muscle.

Donovan pulls my sock off. Surprisingly, the stick itself isn't very bloody and neither is the wound. I direct him to pull a couple damp leaves from a tree. I wipe their moisture against the wound in an effort to clean it some.

"How does it feel?" Donovan asks.

"How do you think?" I say. "But I'll be fine." I ravel my sock around the cut and tie it up as tightly as possible to clot the blood.

"Are you sure?"

I nod.

"What are you even doing out here?" He looks over his shoulder. "Forget it, we don't have time. We can't stay here. Keep close to me. Can you walk? Do you need me to carry you?"

"No. I'm fine."

"Come on," he says. "I don't know who's screwing with me, but they'll find us here for sure."

"Who?"

Donovan takes my hands and helps me up, ignoring my question. He places his arm around my shoulders and aims the flashlight out between us, so I can see as well. We scurry through bushes, over rocks, and between trees—

him, constantly looking over our shoulders to see if we're being followed; me, hobbling as best I can, trying to keep up despite the throb in my foot. We reach a partial clearing and stop to catch our breaths.

"Wait, Donovan," I whisper, finally. I wrap my hand around the protection bottle, still in my coat pocket. With faith, it will protect me. "Go ahead without me if you want." I can't just keep on running. If I want to save Drea, I have to stop and face the future we've created.

He looks at me, a bit confused. "I'm not leaving you in the middle of the woods by yourself. You shouldn't even be out here. Why *are* you?"

"Why are *you* out here?" I ask.

"I had to check something out."

"What?"

"Just something I heard about, all right? So, I headed in this direction, saw something I shouldn't have, and have been running ever since. End of story. I just want to get the hell out of here in one piece."

"Wait, what did you see?"

"Nothing you want to know about now," he says. "Trust me on that."

"Well, I have to check something out too," I say. "And I don't want to run anymore."

"I'll tell you what." He shines his flashlight around until it hits a boulder. "Crouch down behind that rock and I'll make sure they're gone. If everything looks safe, we can both head back to campus." He reaches into his pocket and detaches a penlike flashlight from his key ring. "Hold on to this. I'll be right back. Just try not to make any noise."

I take the flashlight, but I don't sit down. I look up into the cat-black sky, where the tops of trees have parted slightly, allowing me to locate the North Star. I breathe it in, allowing the lights from the star formation and the moon to soak into my face and grant me energy.

And that's when I remember. Donovan's sketchbook in the inner pocket of my jacket. I pull it out, remembering how he said he was sketching last night. I flip to the page, the only night scene in the book. A picture of the last quarter moon.

But the moon tonight is waxing, still days from first quarter. And the first and last quarters are separated by half a month. Impossible for it to change overnight.

I aim the tiny flashlight in the direction of where he headed. Its slender beam allows only a few feet of light. I take careful steps, over brush and fallen leaves, trying my best to be quiet. There seems to be a sort of trail paved through a cluster of trees. I take it, using my most basic instincts as a guide.

I think about doing some last-minute spell, conjuring up some spirit who can answer all my questions. But somehow, deep within me, I already know what I need to. It's like what Gram always said about spells suddenly making sense—how we're the ones who give them meaning, how somewhere deep inside us lies the most powerful truth and will of all.

I lift a delicate, fork-shaped branch from in front of my eyes. And that's when I see it: the construction site from my nightmare. A shell of a house, lit up in the distance by spotlights. It reminds me suddenly of that e-mail Drea got—the one Chad sent her—"The House that Jack Built."

This is where I'll find Drea. I'm sure of it.

The structure of the house is just as I dreamed. Tall, creamy boards have been erected to form walls. A rectangular archway stands at the front as an entrance.

Walking on the ball of my foot now, I move to the front of the house, fearing and knowing exactly what I will find. And there it is. Freshly dug. Drea's name spelled out in the soil.

I want to be sick. I cup my hand up over my mouth and heave in and out. This can't be real. It can't be happening.

But it is.

I feel myself back up, away from the letters, trying to quell my fear as best I can. Seeing these details from my dreams play out in real time is horrible and strange and terrifying all at once. But if I use them the right way, I can possibly save Drea's life.

I run into the house headfirst, my forehead smacking against the spotlight hanging down from the partial roof. A splattering of color-spots shoots in front of my eyes, nearly blinding me. But when the colors fade, I'm able to see. It's just like in my dream, like I've already been here. I stand in a large open area, framed in by tall planks of wood. Ahead of me is a long hallway with adjoining rooms to the left and right.

I take tiny steps across the boards, looking for some sign of Drea. Through a grid of wall planks, I can see a blanket laid out on the floor in the other room, with another spotlight hanging over it. I walk closer. There's a picnic set up. A wicker basket sits in the middle of a red and white checked blanket, with a loaf of French bread and a wine bottle sticking out. An assortment of fresh lilies sprouts from a crystal-cut vase.

Wind combs through the skeleton of the house and distracts me, blows my hair back. My gaze floats over to the corner of the room. A navy blue backpack is slouched against the wall. I approach the bag slowly, as though something alive is lying dormant inside. I pick it up, unzip the main section, and look inside. But it's too dark to see anything clearly.

I sit down with the bag and aim the flashlight into the opening. There's an empty can of Diet Coke. I pull it out, noticing a kiss of salmon-pink lipstick against the rim. Drea's favorite shade. The next item, a half-eaten bar of dark chocolate—the kind Drea always buys from the machine in the dorm lobby—with plastic wrap around the teeth marks for protection. And her physics lab notebook, the one Chad sometimes borrows.

I can see one more item, sitting at the bottom. Its shadow makes a sort of looplike shape against the nylon fabric. I reach my hand in and pull it out. Drea's pink bra, the one that got stolen from the washroom.

My body shakes. I bite down on my tongue to keep from screaming out.

Amber's cell phone rings in my pocket. I answer as quickly as I can get my fingers to work. "Hello?" I whisper, still shaking, barely able to keep the phone in my hands.

"Where the hell are you?"

"Amber—" I gasp, tripping over my breath.

"You were supposed to meet me in my room. The police are here too. I called Officer Tate. We've been here, waiting for you—"

"No, they're coming here. She's coming here. I told her."

"Yeah, well, I told her you were coming to meet me instead. Wait, what's the matter with you? Is something wrong?"

The floorboards creak. I peer in the direction of the main room, noticing that the spotlight has been shut off. Footsteps make their way across the boards in one of the rooms. I click the phone off, stuff everything back into the bag, and jam the flashlight into my pocket. I stand, cemented in the center of the room, hoping the darkness will hide me.

I'm all alone. No one is coming.

thirty-three

The sound of footsteps moving toward me fills my ears. I stretch my arms out and spread my fingers to try and find the doorway that will lead me into the main room, the one I entered. Despite the growing ache, I place all my weight on my bare foot with each step to avoid making noise, but then my ankle makes a loud popping sound.

I close my eyes, clench my fists, and remain still, trying not to breathe. I wait several seconds, but there's only silence.

Slowly, I creep toward the wall and pad my fingers across the planks to try and find the doorway opening. When I do, I stop in what I imagine is the middle of the room, trying to remember whether the front door is to the left or right. The blackness intensifies, shrouding my senses, making my head spin. I want to scream.

The footsteps continue toward me in the darkness, but then they stop; I'm sensing he's just inches away now. I press my body against the planks of wood, trying to squeeze myself through the open gaps to the outside. But it's no use. I can't fit. The only way I'm getting out is through the front door.

"Stacey?"

My chin shakes. Should I speak? Should I answer? I grip the protection bottle so tightly I think the glass might shatter.

"Stacey?" he repeats. "Is that you?"

"Yes."

He clicks the spotlight on over our heads and it takes several seconds before his image is more than a blur of light mixed with black. And then it hits me. The way he's looking at me—head sort of cocked to one side, eyebrows, arched, lips pressed together. It's him. The face in my nightmare. The one I saw but couldn't remember.

Donovan.

The sketch. The phase of the moon. The face in my dream. His constant obsession with Drea, and all the stuff in the backpack. Donovan.

He stands in the middle of the room, just below the spotlight. "You scared the shit out of me," he says. "I went back to look for you, but you were gone and I—are you all right?"

Teeth clenched, jaw stiff, I manage a nod.

"I think the coast is clear if you want to leave," he says.

I nod again, but don't move.

"Well?" he says. "What's wrong?"

I roll my shoulders back and clench the protection bottle, reminding myself of strength and empowerment. "Where's Drea?"

"Drea?" The skin between his eyes gathers in a wrinkle, as though he's genuinely confused.

"I'm not leaving without her."

"You don't want to stay here, Stacey. Trust me. I know we haven't been the best of friends, or even friends for that matter. But you need to trust me on this. It's best if we both leave together. I'll explain when we get back. But like I said before, I'm not leaving you out here alone."

I study his face for some sign of deceit. But his eyes don't flinch once. They stay locked on mine, making me almost believe him. *Almost.*

A bubble of energy explodes in my chest. "Tell me where Drea is. *Now!*"

"I told you, I don't know what you're talking about, but I think you better leave before it's too late."

"Tell me," I say, "or I'm not going anywhere."

"No!" he shouts. He lunges toward me, his hands at my shoulders, and pins me up against the wall.

I grab the protection bottle from my pocket, wrap my hands around the base, and thrust it into his groin—hard. Donovan stumbles back, lets out a short grunt. But it isn't enough. He grabs around my neck and presses the back of my head against a wooden plank.

"Donovan," I gasp, trying to swallow, feeling every muscle in my neck work.

The protection bottle tumbles from my fingers.

His hands lock tighter. Until I can't breathe at all, until my world falls silent.

I feel my lips part, my tongue fall forward, my eyelids twitter.

"Time to go home, *now!*" He releases his grip on my neck and I feel my knees give way. Down to the ground. My hands grasp around my neck. Coughing. Gasping. Trying to fill my lungs with breath.

The protection bottle is lying on the ground just inches away. Still gasping, I reach forward and snag it, and then stand to meet Donovan eye to eye. I can feel the grit of my teeth. I clench the protection bottle and, with all my might, whack it against the side of his head.

Donovan's head snaps back. He yelps and folds to the ground, the flashlight shooting from his hand. I snatch it up and run.

I know it will only be a matter of time before he rebounds and comes looking for me. I reach into my pocket for Amber's cell phone, but it isn't there, just the tiny flashlight. I stop, feel around in my other pockets, pull at the lining. Nowhere. Did I drop it? Stuff it in the backpack by accident?

I continue to run, wiping at the drool from my eyes—tears mixed with cold air. The panting of my breath seems even louder than the breaking of sticks under my feet as I run. It feels like broken glass under my wounded, bare foot, like I might not be able to go on. And then, right below my stomach, a sting, a pulling.

I have to pee.

I aim the flashlight in my random path, its beam illuminating pieces of forest in long and narrow clips. The urge grows more painful with each step. I need to find some place to go. I stop a second, behind a tree, and cross my legs.

I have to trust my body, what it's telling me, where it will lead me. I hold my hand between my legs and fight the urge to give up. What does this mean? What can it tell me? And then it finally hits me—the place my body is propelling me to go is the same place I'll find Drea. S HDN. *She's hidden*. Drea will be hidden inside.

I hobble back in the direction of the construction site. I need to get there, get her out, and flee this forest, before Donovan kills us both.

thirty-four

I find the porta-john—an eight-foot-tall, celery-green, fiber-glass box—just behind the construction site. It's been tipped onto its side.

I prop the flashlight against a rock, on the ground, angling its beam toward me. Then I squat down and feel around the sides of the box. The door faces sideways. I pull at it, noticing a long steel rod wedged into a finger-sized loophole beside the lock on the outer edge of the box. The rod rests over the door crack, pinning the box closed.

"Drea," I whisper into the door crack.

No response.

I pull at the rod, trying to dislodge it out from the loop, the urge to pee now suddenly quelled. "Drea," I whisper again, "can you hear me?" I grip my hands around the rod, hard, but my fingers just slide across the metal with each pull.

I want to cry. I want to be sick. But I can't do either. There isn't time. Drea is depending on me. I have to depend on myself.

I search the ground. There has to be something. A rock. I need a rock. There, in the flashlight's beam, I notice one, about the size of a softball. I pick it up in both hands. Look at it. Feel its ample weight, the nice smooth side.

I squat back down, raise the rock high above my head, and strike the end of the rod. It moves about three inches through the loop. Another foot to go.

I repeat the action, over and over again, watching the rod slowly inch its way from the door crack. Wondering where Donovan is, if he can hear me. The muscles in my arms quiver. Only three more hits. Maybe four. But the next couple times, the rod doesn't seem to budge at all. I close my eyes, try to control my panting, and direct my breath into my arms to give them strength. I raise the rock, one last time, and whack the end of the rod. It skates through the loop. Finally, the door is free.

I throw the door open. There she is. Fetal position. Eyes wide, like a cat. Her hair, tousled and dirty over her face. Thick pieces of duct tape over her mouth, around her wrists and ankles.

The raw, foul stench from the box slaps me across the face, make my stomach wince. I grab her wrists and slide her toward the opening. I can hear her sobbing beneath the tape. Her head quivers, like she's scared and cold at the same time. I grab a corner of the tape, by her ear, and pull until her mouth is free, until her sobs are unleashed.

"Drea," I plead, "you have to keep quiet." I look around. No Donovan yet.

I fumble with the tape around her ankles for the end, where I can pull, but I can't get my fingers to work fast enough. Drea continues to sob—thick, hungry sobs, like she can't get enough breath. She scrunches her knees up and down, like that will release the tape. "Drea," I breathe, "you need to keep still."

I find the end of the tape. I yank on it and start unraveling layer after layer from around her ankles. I glance over my shoulder again. Still clear, though I can sense him getting closer. Drea wriggles her feet back and forth as I get closer to the end. "Stop," I whisper. "You're making it harder."

She wails out even louder. He must have heard us by now.

I free her ankles from the tape, stand up, and grab at her arms to pull her up. She won't budge. Dead weight.

"Drea, come on," I plead.

She focuses down and shakes her head, just keeps on crying.

"Drea, please. I need your help. He's coming, don't you understand? He killed Veronica. We could be next."

She curls her knees into her chest and tightens her eyelids shut to block me out. I take a deep breath in, squat down, place one arm under her knees, the other around her back, and try to pick her up cradle-style.

I wrestle to stand up, putting all the weight in my legs, but the bottom of my foot feels like it's tearing open; there's a burning, itching sensation boring into my arch. I take a step and end up falling down against my back, Drea toppling over me, crying even louder now.

I reach into my pocket for the protection bottle. I position it in her hands and watch her fingers, soiled and bloody at the nubs, wrap around the base.

"Remember strength," I whisper. "And safety."

This seems to calm her a bit. The tears slide down her cheeks with less energy and her eyes cool down into a blank stare.

Straight ahead, just beyond us, I notice a shifting in the bushes. I slide Drea off me and grab the flashlight. I beam the area, but can't see anything. There's only one thing left to do.

I clutch my hands under Drea's arms from behind and start to drag her away, the heels of her boots digging into the earth, as if she's trying to anchor herself in place.

I drag her backwards as fast as I can, trying to check over my shoulder for direction. I search up into the sky for the North Star to make sure I'm leading us back to campus, but the treetops have blocked the view, made it darker. I lead us into an area laden with tall, overgrown bushes.

Drea looks back at me and her mouth arches wide in a scream. Loud. Crazed.

A blade presses against my neck, forcing me to drop her.

"Don't you wish you had gone back to campus, now?" Donovan breathes. He holds me in a headlock, the point of the blade needling into my skin.

"No!" Drea shouts. She lifts her arms toward her head, like she wants to cover her ears, block everything out, but her bound wrists make it impossible.

"Donovan—" The ball in my throat bobs up and down beneath his grip. "Drea—she needs help, a doctor."

"You did this. This is your fault." Donovan releases the headlock and pushes me to the ground; I land smack on my butt. "Hands behind your back!" he shouts.

I comply.

He squats down beside Drea, but keeps one eye on me. He touches the side of her face, the blade brushing against her cheek, and lifts her chin so she'll look at him. "It's okay now. Everything's going to be okay."

Drea shakes her head.

"I had to do this." He rubs her bound wrists. "Don't you understand?" He crouches down even further to study her—her red, runny eyes, the dried-up veins of black mascara that bleed down her cheeks, the bits of dirt that surround her pasty, white mouth, the way she's rocking back and forth, crying, gasping for breath. "I had to tie you up like this; you said you wanted to leave. I had to make you listen; I had to make you understand."

There's a long, forklike branch lying just beyond reach. Focusing on Donovan, I sit up tall, lengthening my spine, trying to inch myself toward it.

"I love you, Drea," Donovan continues. "That's why I planned all this. The house, the picnic, the lilies." He smiles, as though the explanation will give her pleasure. "I only hid you because I didn't want anyone to find you. Don't you understand how that would have ruined everything? If you come back to the house with me again I can show you all I've planned. I'll show you the place where I dug out your name, where I've planted lily bulbs that will spell out the letters."

Drea's breathing is getting worse, wheezing, the more he talks to her.

"Donovan," I say, "I know you want what's best for her. But she's freezing. She's having trouble breathing. She needs a doctor."

"No!" Donovan shouts. He points the blade toward my face and his hand shakes with rage. "Not until she understands." He focuses back on her but keeps the blade pointed at me, midair. "I'll take care of her. I'm the only one who knows how."

I stretch my leg out and try to reach the branch with my foot.

"I love you, Drea." He pats the side of her face. "And I know you love me too. I know you used to love talking to me . . . on the phone—our long conversations." His eyes, teary and desperate, await her response, her affirmation.

Drea's crying gets louder, more forceful with each breath. She huddles deeper into her crouch and continues to rock back and forth.

"What's the matter with you?" Donovan shouts. "Why won't you say anything? Why won't she say anything?" He turns to glare at me over the blade.

"You killed Veronica," I say. "You called her and sent her notes and lilies, just like Drea."

Donovan shakes his head. "It was an accident. She took my idea for a surprise and twisted it all around for her own needs." Donovan stabs the knife into the earth repeatedly. "She wanted to scare you, Drea. She wanted to pretend that she was getting stalked and then disappear, so you'd think something really bad happened to her. She thought that if you got scared enough, you'd leave campus and she'd be able to have Chad."

I watch the knife plunge into the dirt over and over again, watch his shoulders; wonder if I'd be able to lunge at him, hold his arm down. I inch myself to the left, closer to the branch.

His eyes remain focused on Drea, on trying to convince her. "I had to stop her, Drea," he continues. "I didn't want to do what I did. You have to believe me. I'm not like that. You know I'm not like that. She wanted to scare you into leaving school. Don't you understand? I couldn't let her do that."

He continues to stab at the ground, the blade getting closer and closer to his knee. It's almost like he really does love her. Or at least he thinks he does. So maybe that's what my nightmares were trying to tell me. Maybe love really is funny—funny strange. Maybe even bizarre. I glance at Drea, still rocking back and forth, her eyes still blank.

Donovan takes a breath and plunges the blade down into his knee, penetrating the skin, drawing a gash of blood. He removes the knife with a slight flinch but contin-ues stabbing the ground, like it doesn't matter, like he doesn't feel it. He wants Drea to answer him, to tell him that everything will be happily ever after. I'm not even sure she's listening.

Using the ball of my foot, I slowly guide the branch inward, bending my knee just slightly to get it closer, the blood sopping through my sock now.

"She was no good, Drea," Donovan pleads. "She said you were a slut."

I break my hands from the clasp behind my back. The branch is now within reach. I grab it and Donovan notices.

"What are you doing?" he shouts.

I stand up and swing the branch at Donovan's knife-holding hand. But instead of dropping it, he intercepts the swing and nabs the branch from me.

He gets up, breaks the branch over his knee in two places, and throws the pieces to the side.

I look around for something else to protect myself. A rock, over to the right. I move toward it but Donovan grabs me, shoves my back up against a tree. He clasps my wrists together in his hand, holds them over my head, and presses the knife against my cheek. "You think you're smarter than I am, don't you? Don't you?"

I shake my head.

He draws a line with the blade down my cheek, over my chin, and then points the tip into my throat.

"No!" Drea screams.

I look over Donovan's shoulder. Drea is standing, her fingers tightly woven together, wrapped around the protection bottle.

Donovan takes a step back to look at her. "Drea?"

"No!" she cries, shaking her head.

Donovan's grip on my hands loosens. "Drea?" His hips angle in her direction. He releases my hands but keeps me pinned with the knife.

I let my arms fall gradually, grab his knife-holding hand, and bite it—hard, through the skin. He lets out a deep, throaty wail and drops the knife.

"Drea!" I shout.

She grapples for the knife and gets it, holds it tightly in her hands with the protection bottle.

"Give it to me, Drea," I say.

Instead she points the blade at him.

Donovan extends his arms toward her, like he wants to calm her down, take the knife. "Drea," he says. "Be careful with that. You don't know what you're doing."

"No!" Drea breathes, the knife shaking in her grip. "Down. Sit down."

Donovan motions to sit, but then lurches at her, grabs her wrist, and squeezes the knife right out of her hands.

His back facing me, I take a step toward him, position myself sideways to kick out with my sneakered foot, and plunge my heel with all my strength into the back of his leg. The knife jumps from his grip. He falls to his knees. I move to grab the knife, just before his fingers snatch it up.

"Hold it." These are the words that flash across my mind, but it isn't me who says them. I look up.

It's Officer Tate. She emerges from a nest of trees opposite us and leads a few other officers in our direction. She walks straight toward me. "Drop the knife and step back," she says.

I do, knowing that finally we're safe.

Officer Tate wraps a pair of silver cuffs around Donovan's wrists and reads him his rights. Another officer removes his own jacket and wraps it around Drea's shoulders. He motions to grab the protection bottle from her grip, but she pulls away. Instead he just unwinds the tape from her wrists.

I kind of just stand there, taking it all in, relieved I don't have to fight anymore.

Donovan takes one last look at Drea before Officer Tate escorts him away.

It's the same kind of look he always gives her—intense and longing, like he really believes he loves her. Like he'll be back one day to prove how much.

I walk over to Drea and hug her.

"I'm sorry," she says.

"I'm sorry too."

I close my eyes and press her into me, feel her fingers touch my back, then press against me to return the hug. For just a moment, I imagine Maura in my arms.

"Thank you," I whisper into her ear.

"Thank *you*," she whispers back.

I shake my head, grateful that Drea is safe, but also grateful that my real nightmare has finally ended.

thirty-five

Three months later—just before February vacation and just after the trial. Drea has come back to campus to testify. She ended up going home immediately after Donovan's arrest and spent the time getting herself back together and trying to make sense of what doesn't seem possible.

Now that she's back and things have somewhat settled, Amber, Chad, PJ, and I have planned a sort of get-together at the Hangman Café.

No one seems surprised that it was Donovan stalking Drea. Everyone knew how crazy he was for her—literally. The only surprising part for most is that Veronica really was involved, that a ridiculous plan to get some guy could result in her own death.

It turns out I was right to be suspicious of Veronica's stalker story. Like Donovan said, Veronica wasn't getting stalked at all. But she heard Drea was and wanted to scare her. Basically, she was supposed to be leaving campus to go on a two-week safari with her parents, a trip she conveniently failed to tell Drea or anyone about. Not so coincidentally, she was supposed to be leaving for the trip the morning after she said the stalker was coming for her. In a nutshell, she wanted Drea to go completely freakazoid and either flip out or leave campus when she thought Veronica was taken—a foreshadowing, basically, of what would happen to her.

Totally and completely sad.

But just as sad is that Donovan got completely pissed when the scuttlebutt about Veronica and Drea getting stalked by the same person got to him. He was the one who stuffed the MIND YOUR OWN BUSINESS note, along with Drea's handkerchief, into Veronica's mailbox. It turns out Donovan included Drea's hanky with the note as a sort of signature token—so Veronica would know it was from Drea's stalker, so she'd take it seriously and drop her whole stalker story. Giving Veronica the hanky also put Drea's possession into Veronica's room. So, as the prosecuting attorney suggested, if something happened to Drea, Donovan would have someone to pin it on.

Twistedly clever, I suppose.

The note and hanky did work in freaking Veronica out, which is why she told us she no longer wanted anything to do with the whole stalking business. But, unfortunately, the scuttlebutt didn't die. Which only pissed Donovan off even more. Using Chad's e-mail account, just like he used it to send Drea "The House that Jack Built" e-mail, he lured Veronica into the school to confront her about her stalking tales, but ended up killing her—by accident, he swore.

And the jury believed him.

They also believed him when he said he never intended to physically harm Drea. The stalking, as he and his lawyer asserted, was a way for him to get close to Drea. And, when Drea seemed okay to talk to his mysterious phone-caller persona, Donovan started to confuse their relationship and got all possessive about it, including getting angry and jealous when she made plans with Chad. He was the one who took Chad's hockey jersey from our window that night, who stuffed it into Chad's mailbox along with the STAY AWAY FROM HER. I'M WATCHING YOU note. He was also the one who stole our laundry from the washroom. When he saw Drea's hanky and bra sitting atop the heap, he just collected it all, in hopes of finding more Drea relics to add to his collection.

On the night that Drea was taken, after the hospital, when Amber and PJ dropped her off in front of the dorm, Donovan was waiting for her. He told her he needed to talk about something and so they went for a walk. Basically, he brought her to the construction site, his idea of a romantic place, and professed his undying love for her. She got weirded out and ended up telling him she wanted to go back to the dorm.

Donovan said no, nabbed her, but then freaked and didn't know what to do when she didn't seem pleased with his plans for happily-ever-after—hence the defense that his actions weren't premeditated.

The lilies, ironically, were chosen simply because Donovan liked them and thought their charm and elegance best represented Drea. And "The House that Jack Built" e-mail was just a little riddle, a foreshadowing basically of the romantic rendezvous he had planned for them.

When he saw me in the woods the next night in search of Drea, he panicked and made up that bogus story about someone following us and not being able to get his cell phone to work. Afraid that I might spot Drea at the construction site, he told me to stay put, made up that excuse about checking things out, and then went and hid Drea in the porta-john.

In the end, he was charged with involuntary manslaughter, labeled temporarily insane, and sent to a juvenile detention center for mentally disturbed boys. Still, freedom only five years away, on his twenty-first birthday, just doesn't seem fitting. Veronica will be dead forever.

After the arrest, Officer Tate gave me this big, long lecture about getting involved where I have no business, how dangerous it was that I went into the forest by myself, and how I could have jeopardized everything, including the case. But then she also thanked me, told me how brave I am, and promised she'd never underestimate natural human instinct again.

Neither will I.

So now, after the trial, the school has agreed to accommodate us by allowing the Hangman to be closed for our private farewell, and supplying us with unlimited café fare.

We've decorated the room as cheerfully as possible. Chad and PJ have hung pink and yellow streamers around the perimeter while Amber and I have layered, bunched, and twisted pieces of crepe paper together to make roses as centerpiece decorations. The school is even letting us borrow the helium machine to fill balloons that we've tied to everyone's chair.

It isn't a surprise party; it's just an opportunity for all of us to get together before Drea goes back. She's going to spend the rest of the school year at home, with private tutors and in family counseling, then come back for senior year.

I know I'm going to miss her more than anything, but at least I won't have to room by myself. Madame Discharge has agreed to let Amber move in. That is, Amber says, if I stop my nasty bedwetting. But I haven't had an accident, or a nightmare, since the day before Veronica's death.

"Did we get her a parting gift?" PJ asks, his voice all high on helium.

"Good thing we didn't count on you for that," Amber says, stuffing her sweater with two balloons, admiring her busty profile in the window reflection. "What do you think?" She points the balloons in his direction and arches her back for show.

"Ain't nothing like the real thing, baby," he sings, then blows her a kiss.

Amber smiles and removes the balloons. The two of them have been spending a lot of time together these past few weeks, like the tension of the trial has bonded them in some way, made them realize what's really important. I think it's done that for all of us.

For Drea's going-away gift, we pooled our money to buy her a brand-new diary, like a new start on life, and a five-pound box of Godiva chocolates, just in case of emergency. I also wrapped up the protection bottle, still intact.

"She's here!" Chad shouts.

Chad's really been great during this whole ordeal. He went to the trial every day, called Drea every night at her hotel, even took extra notes and kept track of class assignments while she was at home—classes he doesn't even take. What's surprising, even to myself, is that it didn't make me jealous. It just made me realize more significantly what an amazing person he is.

"Oh my god!" Drea yelps on her way in. "You guys didn't have to do all this."

"Stacey made us," PJ says, running his fingers over his cherry-red hair spikes.

We spend the next couple hours laughing and joking about all our fun times, before the stuff with Donovan ever started. Chad brings up the time when me, Drea, and Amber snuck out of the dorm after hours and went to the movies, dressed in our pajamas. And then PJ does an impersonation of each of us—Amber, Princess Wedge-picker; Chad, Master Slacker; Drama Queen Drea; and me, Psychic Friend, mostly likely to open up my own twenty-four-hour hotline. Of course we reciprocate the attention, making fun of his hair and his disgusting lunch concoctions.

After Drea has opened her gifts and the last gingerbread cookie is eaten, PJ and Amber kiss Drea goodbye and shuffle off alone together, holding hands.

Chad turns to Drea. "I can walk you out."

"Can you just give Stacey and me a second?" Drea asks.

He nods, collecting a stack of dirty plates off the table and bringing them out back.

Drea focuses on the protection bottle in her hands.

"So you'll always be safe," I say.

We hug—a long, full squeeze—and try our best not to cry.

"I'll come visit this summer," I say.

Drea nods and looks toward the kitchen, where Chad is stacking dishes. "He's a great guy, you know."

"I know."

"He thinks you're pretty great too," she says. "He told me. He's always telling me. We've spent a lot of time together these past few weeks, him and me. It's been good just being friends. Easier. Better. And as both of your friends, I think you guys owe it to yourselves to give it a try."

"Drea?!" A nervous, gurglelike laugh bubbles up from my throat.

"I love you both." She leans forward and kisses my cheek.

.   .   .

Chad helps carry Drea's last few bags into her parents' car, parked and waiting just outside. We stand outside, saying our last good-byes, promising to call, e-mail, and visit. And then her parents drive her away.

And there's just Chad and me.

"So," he says, "I guess it's just the two of us."

"I guess so."

He holds out his hand and I take it, and it feels like Christmas inside my palm—all warm and tingly.

We walk past the Hangman, ignoring the mess inside, like cleaning up now would really put an end to the day, the last thing either of us wants. We find ourselves taking a turn by the tree where we kissed that first time, and sit down beneath it.

I lean back against the trunk and inhale the breath of winter—cool, fresh, and awakening. It makes me feel beautiful. The way the wind blows my hair back. The smell of bark, mixed with the chill in the air. It makes me happy to be going home for February vacation. Happy to take a break. To see Mom again. To start fresh.

"What are you thinking?" Chad asks.

"How happy I am," I say. "And about déjà vu."

"Déjà vu?"

"You know. Already been seen. You and me, here again."

"So, I guess for this to be true déjà vu, I'd have to kiss you again."

I nod, but this time it's me who kisses him. A five-alarm, hot wasabe, sexilicious kiss.

We kiss some more, and talk and laugh, until well after dark, when the full moon has made its appearance and the brightest star has gone to bed behind the clouds.

I feel stronger now than ever before. Not because of Chad and finding ourselves under this tree again. Not because of saving Drea, or seeing Donovan put away. But because I know that no matter how many nightmares I'll have in the future, I can finally trust myself.

THE END

ACKNOWLEDGMENTS

I want to first thank members of my writing group—Lara Zeises, Steven Goldman, and Tea Benduhn—who have supported and encouraged me throughout numerous drafts of this novel. Your friendship, advice, and thorough critiques have truly been invaluable to me. They've helped make *Blue* a better novel and me a better writer.

Ed, I think you must have read at least ninety-seven drafts of this novel. I can't thank you enough for your friendship, love, patience, and support.

I've been fortunate to have some truly inspiring teachers. Thanks to Lisa Jahn-Clough for her advice and encouragement and for helping to nurture my love of young adult literature and writing. Also thanks to Jessica Treadway for her support and enthusiasm for *Blue*. Finally, thanks to Dr. MaryKay Mahoney, who encouraged and believed in my writing in its early stages. I truly believe that if it wasn't for that encouragement, I may never have seriously pursued my passion for writing.

Thanks to Llewellyn editors Megan Atwood and Becky Zins, who have offered such helpful editorial advice, thorough comments, and enthusiasm for *Blue*, and who believe enough in Stacey and her gang to see them through a sequel.

Thanks to the many other friends and family members who have read pieces and/or drafts of this novel in all its many stages: Mom, Lee Ann, Delia, Sara, Haig, and everyone in Lisa's YA classes.

Thanks to Lieutenant Fran Hart of the Burlington, Massachusetts, Police Department for answering all my police-related questions for *Blue*. Also thanks to Dr. Kathryn Rexrode, M.D. for answering the medical-related questions.

Finally, thanks to my mother for her endless love and support, who taught me how to read the cards and passed down some of the tales and home remedies of her mother and the generations of women before her.